Praise for *The Same Sea*

"This lovely, lyrical territory, irrigated by numerous streams of consciousness, reminded me of some of the great things a novel can do. It can cast us into a dream state, put us into contact with our beloved dead and help us recognize the hidden connections among all people and all things."　—*Chicago Tribune*

"[It] grips the reader with its narrative drive and vivid, fascinating characters like a combination of literary experiment and wildly successful thriller....Amos Oz has written a profound and beautiful book."　—*The Jewish Quarterly*

"Deeply original and, in its quiet way, deeply ambitious...This novel is about Israel, loss and the need for search. But its meditations on personal loss are as archetypal as the ancient Hebrew on which it draws."　—*The Times* (London)

"This is vintage Mr. Oz, arguably his best work ever."　—*The Washington Times*

"*The Same Sea* is at once spare and lushly experimental, an unusual mixture of hard, precise prose that drives the story forward and often lyrical, evocative verse that bathes us in mental glow of each of the characters."　—*The Nation*

"Very few works of fiction are written with such economy, simplicity and precision...Oz has written many works of fiction, poetry and political commentary. But if these were his only lines they would be worthy indeed."
　—*The Sunday Telegraph* (London)

"Oz has a gift for uncovering layers of meaning in the routines of daily life, and the narrative is enriched by allusions to Ecclesiastes and the Song of Songs as well as to modern Hebrew literature.... A defining work from a writer of major significance." —Library Journal

"Elegant... Oz takes a fresh tack in this searching playlike tale told alternately in radiant verse and meditative prose. Richly embroidered, sweetly erotic, and lyrically philosophical." —*Booklist*

"Never has the author's writing been more controlled and polished.... An eloquent and thoughtful exposition, of human nature, the power of words and the stories they tell." —*The Times Literary Supplement* (London)

"Amos Oz has written a truly bold and innovative novel that attains some of the peaks of beauty and wisdom.... A wise, confessional, poetic, crazy book."
—*Ha'lr* (Israel)

The Same Sea

BY AMOS OZ

Fiction

My Michael
Elsewhere, Perhaps
Touch the Water, Touch the Wind
Unto Death
The Hill of Evil Counsel
Where the Jackals Howl
A Perfect Peace
Black Box
To Know A Woman
Fima
Don't Call It Night
Panther in the Basement

Nonfiction

The Story Begins
In the Land of Israel
The Slopes of Lebanon
Under This Blazing Light
Israel, Palestine & Peace

For children

Soumchi

AMOS OZ

The Same Sea

Translated from the Hebrew by
Nicholas de Lange
in collaboration with the author

A HARVEST BOOK
HARCOURT, INC.
San Diego   New York   London

This is a translation of *Oto Ha-Yam*

Library of Congress Cataloging-in-Publication Data
Oz, Amos.
[Oto ha-yam. English]
The same sea/Amos Oz; translated from the Hebrew by Nicholas de Lange
in collaboration with the author.
p.   cm.
ISBN 0-15-100572-9
ISBN 0-15-601312-6 (pbk)
I. De Lange, N. R. M. (Nicholas Robert Michael), 1944–   II. Title.
PJ5054.O9 O8613 2001
892.4'36—dc21   2001024121

Text set in Centaur MT
Designed by Linda Lockowitz

First Harvest edition 2002
K J I H G F E D C B A

Printed in the United States of America

A Note on Pronunciation

One point that was impossible to convey in the translation: the name "Albert"
is pronounced as in French (with a silent t) by everyone except Bettine, who
pronounces it as it is written, with the stress on the second syllable.

Nicholas de Lange

The Same Sea

A cat

Not far from the sea, Mr. Albert Danon
lives in Amirim Street, alone. He is fond
of olives and feta; a mild accountant, he lost
his wife not long ago. Nadia Danon died one morning
of ovarian cancer, leaving some clothes,
a dressing table, some finely embroidered
place mats. Their only son, Enrico David,
has gone off mountaineering in Tibet.

Here in Bat Yam the summer morning is hot and clammy
but on those mountains night is falling. Mist
is swirling low in the ravines. A needle-sharp wind
howls as though alive, and the fading light
looks more and more like a nasty dream.

At this point the path forks:
one way is steep, the other gently sloping.
Not a trace on the map of the fork in the path.
And as the evening darkens and the wind lashes him
with sharp hailstones, Rico has to guess
whether to take the shorter or the easier way down.

Either way, Mr. Danon will get up now
and switch off his computer. He will go
and stand by the window. Outside in the yard
on the wall is a cat. It has spotted a lizard. It will not let go.

A bird

Nadia Danon. Not long before she died a bird
on a branch woke her.
At four in the morning, before it was light, *narimi*
narimi said the bird.

What will I be when I'm dead? A sound or a scent
or neither. I've started a mat.
I may still finish it. Dr. Pinto
is optimistic: the situation is stable. The left one
is a little less good. The right one is fine. The X-rays are clear. See
for yourself: no secondaries here.

At four in the morning, before it is light, Nadia Danon
begins to remember. Ewes' milk cheese. A glass of wine.
A bunch of grapes. A scent of slow evening on the Cretan hills,
the taste of cold water, the whispering of pines, the shadow
of the mountains spreading over the plain, *narimi*
narimi the bird sang there. I'll sit here and sew.
I'll be finished by morning.

Details

Rico David was always reading. He thought the world
was in a bad way. The shelves are covered with piles of his books,
pamphlets, papers, publications, on all sorts
of wrongs: black studies, women's studies,
lesbians and gays, child abuse, drugs, race,
rain forests, the hole in the ozone layer, not to mention injustice
in the Middle East. Always reading. He read everything. He went
to a left-wing rally with his girlfriend Dita Inbar.
Left without saying a word. Forgot to call. Came home late. Played his guitar.

Your mother begs you, his father pleaded. She's not feeling too—
and you're making it worse. Rico said, OK, give me a break.
But how can anyone be so insensitive? Forgetting to switch off.
Forgetting to close. Forgetting to get back before three in the morning.

Dita said: Mr. Danon, try to see it his way.
It's painful for him too. Now you're making him feel guilty;
after all, it's not his fault she's dead. He has a right
to a life of his own. What did you expect him to do? Sit holding her hand?
Life goes on. One way or another everyone gets left
alone. I'm not much for this trip to Tibet
either, but still, he's entitled to try to find himself. Especially after
losing his mother. He'll be back, Mr. Danon, but don't hang around
waiting for him. Do some work, get some exercise, whatever. I'll drop by
sometime.

And since then he goes out to the garden at times. Prunes the roses.
Ties up the sweet peas. Inhales the smell of the sea from afar,
salt, seaweed, the warm dampness. He might
call her tomorrow. But Rico forgot to leave her number
and there are dozens of Inbars in the phone book.

Later, in Tibet

One summer morning, when he was young, he and his mother took the bus
from Bat Yam to Jaffa, to see his Aunt Clara.
The night before he refused to sleep: he was afraid the alarm clock
would stop in the night, and he wouldn't wake. And what if
it rains, or if we are late.

Between Bat Yam and Jaffa a donkey cart
had overturned. Smashed watermelons on the asphalt,
a blood bath. Then the fat driver took offense
and shouted at another fat man, with greased hair. An old lady
yawned at his mother. Her mouth was a grave, empty and deep.
On a bench at a stop sat a man in a tie and white shirt, wearing
his jacket over his knees. He wouldn't board the bus.
Waved it on. Maybe he was waiting
for another bus. Then they saw a squashed cat. His mother
pressed his head to her tummy: don't look, you'll cry out again
in your sleep. Then a girl with her head shaved: lice? Her crossed leg
almost revealed a glimpse. And an unfinished building and dunes of sand.
An Arab coffee house. Wicker stools. Smoke,
acrid and thick. Two men bending forward, heads almost touching.

A ruin. A church. A fig tree. A bell.
A tower. A tiled roof. Wrought-iron grilles. A lemon tree.
The smell of fried fish. And between two walls
a sail and a sea rocking.

Then an orchard, a convent, palm trees,
date palms perhaps, and shattered buildings; if you continue
along this road you eventually reach
south Tel Aviv. Then the Yarkon.
Then citrus groves. Villages. And beyond
the mountains. And after that it is already
night. The uplands of Galilee. Syria. Russia.
Or Lapland. The tundra. Snowy steppes.

Later, in Tibet, more asleep than awake,
he remembers his mother. If we don't wake up
we've had it. We'll be late. In the snow in the tent in the sleeping-bag
he stretches to press his head to her tummy.

Calculations

In Amirim Street Mr. Danon is still awake.
It's two in the morning. On the screen before him
the figures don't add up. Some company
or other. A mistake
or a fraud? He checks. Can't spot anything. On an embroidered mat
the tin clock ticks. He puts on his coat and goes out. It's six now
in Tibet. A smell of rain but no rain in the street in Bat Yam.
Which is empty. Silent. Blocks of flats. A mistake
or a fraud. Tomorrow we'll see.

A mosquito

Dita slept with a good friend
of Rico's, Giggy Ben-Gal. He got on her nerves
when he called screwing intercourse. He disgusted her
by asking her afterwards how good it had been
for her on a scale of zero to a hundred. He had an opinion
about everything. He started yammering on about the female orgasm
being less physical, more emotional. Then he discovered
a fat mosquito on her shoulder. He squashed it, brushed it off, rustled
the local paper and fell asleep
on his back. Arms spread out in a cross.
Leaving no room for her. His cock shrivelled too
and went to sleep with a mosquito on it: blood vengeance.

She took a shower. Combed her hair. Put on a black T-shirt that Rico
had left in one of her drawers. Less. Or more. Emotional. Physical.
Sexy. Bullshit. Sensual. Sexual.
Opinions night and day. That's wrong. That's right. What's squashed
can't be unsquashed. I should go and see how the old man's doing.

It's hard

With the first rays of dawn he opens his eyes. The mountain range looks like
a woman, powerful, serene, asleep on her side after a night of love.
A gentle breeze, satisfying itself, stirs the flap of his tent.
Swelling, billowing, like a warm belly. Rising and falling.

With the tip of his tongue he touches the dip in the middle of his left hand,
at the innermost point of his palm. It feels
like the touch of a nipple, soft and hard.

Alone

An arrow poised on a taut bow: he remembers the line
of the slope of her thigh. He guesses her hips' movement towards him.
He gathers himself. Crawls out of his sleeping-bag. Fills
his lungs with snowy air. A pale, opaline
mist is rolling slowly upwards: a filmy nightdress on the curve
of the mountain.

A suggestion

In Bostros Street in Jaffa there lives a Greek man who reads fortunes in cards.
A sort of clairvoyant. They say he even calls up the dead. Not
with glasses and Ouija boards
but visibly. Only for a moment, though, and in a dim light,
and you can't talk and you can't touch. Then death takes over again.

Bettine Carmel, a chartered accountant, told Albert. She is a deputy inspector
on the Property Tax Board. When she has a moment he is invited to her flat
for herbal tea and a chat, about the children, life,
things in general. He has been widowed since the early summer,
she has been a widow for twenty years now. She is sixty
and so is he. Since his wife died he has not looked
at another woman. But each time they talk
it brings them both a feeling of peace. Albert, she says, why don't you go
and see him some time. It really helped me. It's probably an illusion, but
just for a moment Avram came back. It's four hundred shekels and no
guarantee. If nothing happens, the money's gone. People pay even more
for experiences that touch them much less. No illusions
is a current catchphrase which in my view is just a cliché:
even if you live to be a hundred, you never stop searching
for those long dead.

Nadia looks

A framed photograph stands on the sideboard: her chestnut hair
pinned up. Her eyes are a little too round, which is possibly why
her face expresses surprise or doubt, as though asking: What, really?
It's not in the picture, but Albert remembers what pinning
her hair up did to her. It let you observe, if you wished,
the soft, fine, fragrant down on the nape of her neck.

In the photograph hanging in their bedroom Nadia looks
different. More worldly. Fine earrings, a hint of a shy smile
which both promises and asks for
more time: not now. Later, whatever you want.

Rico looks

Kind-heartedness, bitterness, stamina, scorn—these are what Mr. Danon sees
on the face of his son in the photo. Like a double exposure: the clear, open
brow and eyes are at odds with the wry,
almost cynical line of the lips. In the picture the uniform broadens the span
of his shoulders, transforming the boy into a tough man. For several years
it's been almost impossible to talk to him. What's new? Nothing special.
How are you? Not too bad. Have you eaten? Have you
had a drink? Would you like
a piece of chicken? Give me a break, Dad. I'm all right.
And what do you think about the peace talks? He mumbles some wisecrack,
already halfway out the door. Bye. And don't work too hard.
But still there is a kind of affection, not in the words, not in the photo,
but in between or beside. His hand on my arm: its touch
is calm, intimate yet not really. And now in Tibet
it is almost twenty to three. Instead of investigating further
what's missing from the picture I'll make some toast, drink some tea,
and then get down to work. There's something wrong with this photo.

On the other side

A postcard arrived, with a green stamp: Hi Dad, it's nice here, high and bright,
the snow reminds me of Bulgaria in the bedtime stories Mom used to tell
about villages with wells and forests with goblins (though here there are
almost no trees; only shrubs grow at this altitude, and even they appear to do
so out of sheer stubbornness). I'm fine here, got my sweater and everything,
and some Dutch guys are with me—they're really safety-conscious. And by
the way, the thin air somehow
totally changes every sound. Even the most terrifying shout
doesn't break the silence but instead, how can I put this, joins it. Now
don't you sit up working too late. PS On the other side
you can see a picture of a ruined village. A thousand years or so ago
there was a civilisation here that was lost without trace. Nobody knows
what happened.

All of a sudden

Early next evening Dita turned up. Light-footed, out of breath, unannounced
she rang his doorbell, waited. No use, he's not in, just my luck.
When she had given up and was on her way downstairs she met him coming up,
carrying a string bag full of shopping. She grabbed one handle
and so, embarrassed, hands touching, they stood on the stairs. At first
he was a little startled when she tried to take the bag away from him:
for a moment he didn't recognize her, with her
short hair, and her cheeky skirt that almost wasn't there. The reason
I came is that I got a postcard this morning.
He sat her down in the living room. He told her at once
that he too had had a postcard from Tibet. She showed him.
He showed her. They compared. Then she followed him into the kitchen.
Helped him unload the shopping, and put it away. Mr. Danon
put the kettle on. While they waited they sat facing one another
at the kitchen table. One knee over the other, in her orange skirt,
she seemed almost naked. But she's so young. Still a child. Quickly he
averted his gaze. He had trouble asking her whether she and Rico were still
or no longer. He chose his words carefully, tactfully evasive. Dita laughed: I'm
not his, I never was, and he isn't mine, and anyway, you see,
those are just labels. Everyone for themselves. I'm allergic
to anything permanent or fixed. It's better to just let everything flow. Trouble is,
that's a kind of fixed notion too. As soon as you define, it's a mess. Look,
the kettle's boiling. Don't get up, Albert, let me see to it. Coffee or tea?
She stood up, sat down, and saw he was blushing. She found it sweet. She
crossed her legs again, straightened her skirt, more or less. By the way, I need
your advice as a tax consultant. It's like this: I've written a screenplay,
it's going into production, and I've some papers to sign. Don't be mad at me

for taking the opportunity to ask you, just like that. You mustn't feel obliged. On the contrary, I'll be delighted:

he started to give her a detailed explanation, not as to a client, more to a daughter. As he clarified things from various angles, his docile body began suddenly to strain at the bit.

Olives

Sometimes the taste of these strong olives cured slowly in oil,
with cloves of garlic, bay leaves and chillies and lemon and salt,
conjures a whiff of a bygone age: rocky crannies,
goats, shade and the sound of pipes,
the tune of the breath of primeval times. The chill of a cave, a hidden cottage
in a vineyard, a lodge in a garden, a slice of barley bread and well water.
You are from there. You have lost your way.
Here is exile. Your death will come, and lay a knowing hand on your shoulder.
Come, it's time to go home.

Sea

There is a village in a valley. Twenty flat-roofed huts. Mountain light,
sharp and intense. In a bend in the stream the six climbers, mostly Dutchmen,
are sprawled on a groundsheet, playing cards. Paul cheats a little, and Rico,
who is out, retires, swaddled in anorak and scarf, slowly inhaling
the crisp mountain air. He lifts up his eyes: sharp sickle peaks.
A couple of cirrus clouds. A redundant midday moon.
And if you lose your footing, the chasm has a womblike smell.
His knee aches and the sea is calling.

Fingers

Stavros Evangelides, an eighty-year-old Greek wearing a crumpled brown suit
with a stain above the left knee, has a bald brown head patterned with wrinkles,
moles and grey bristles, and a prominent nose, but perfect, young teeth,
and large, joyful eyes: guileless eyes, which seem to see only good. His room
is shabby. The curtains are faded. There's a crooked wooden shutter
secured on the inside with a bar. And a thick blend
of sepia smells heavily overlaid with incense. The walls are covered
with icons, and an oil lamp illuminates a Crucifixion with a very young
Christ, as though the painter has brought Golgotha forward,
so that the miracle of the loaves and the fishes, and the raising of Lazarus
must have occurred after the Resurrection. Mr. Evangelides is
a slow man. He seats his visitor, goes out and comes back twice,
the second time bringing a glass of water,
lukewarm. First he collects his fee, in cash, counting the money methodically,
and enquires politely who it was in fact
who recommended the gentleman to him. His Hebrew is simple but correct,
with a slight Arab accent. Are his perfect teeth his own?
Impossible to tell for the moment. Then he asks a few general questions
about life, health and so on. He takes an interest
in Albert's family and country of origin. He maintains that the Balkans belong
both to the west and to the east. He writes all the answers down in detail
in a notebook. He wants to know about those who have gone before,
who and how and when. And who is the deceased who has brought you here
this evening, sir? Then he ponders. Digests. Studies his fingers
for a while, as though mentally checking to make sure they are all present
and correct. He explains modestly that he cannot guarantee
results. A man and a woman, you must surely know, sir,

are a mysterious union: one day they are close, the next
they turn their backs. I must ask you to breathe normally, sir.
Palms up. Clear your mind. That's right. Now we can begin.
The visitor closes his eyes to remember. *Narimi narimi* the bird said to her.
Then he reopens them. The room is empty.
The light is grey-brown. For a moment he fancies he can make out
an embroidered pattern in the folds of the curtains.

Some time later Mr. Evangelides came back into the room. Tactfully
he refrained from asking how it went. He brought
another glass of water, this time cool and fresh. A pleasant, soothing light
shone from his smiling eyes between the brown wrinkles, the smile
of a bright child displaying milk-white teeth. Treading softly
he saw his visitor to the door. The following day over herbal tea at the office
Bettine said to him, Albert, don't take it to heart, one way or another
almost everybody ends up disappointed. That's the way it is.
He was in no hurry to reply. For some time he studied
his fingers. After I left, he said, just like that in the middle of the street
I saw someone who looked a bit like her. From behind.

You can hear

Bettine sits alone at home after midnight in an armchair reading a novel
about loneliness and wrongdoing. Someone, a secondary character, dies
because of a misdiagnosis. She lays the book
face down in her lap, and thinks about Albert: Why
did I send him to the Greek? I caused him unnecessary pain. And yet
we have nothing to lose, after all. He is living all by himself now,
and I am on my own too. You can hear the sea out there.

A shadow

Vague rumors abound, and half-testimonies too, concerning a gigantic,
almost human creature, that roams alone in the Tibetan mountains.
Single and free. Footprints have been photographed in the snow
once or twice in inaccessible places where even the most intrepid
mountaineer would hardly dare venture. Almost certainly
it is nothing but a local legend. Like the Loch Ness monster
or the ancient Cyclops. His mother, who sat embroidering
almost to the hour of her death, his sad, withdrawn father
who sits night after night at his computer looking for loopholes
in the tax laws, everyone in fact, is condemned to wait
for their own death locked in a separate cage. You too, with your travelling,
your obsession to go further and further away and hoard more
and more experiences, are carting your own cage around with you
to the outer edge of the zoo. Everyone has their own captivity. The bars
separate everyone from everyone else. If that solitary snowman really exists,
without sex or partner, without birth or progeny or death,
roaming these mountains for a thousand years,
light and naked, how it must laugh as it moves among the cages.

Through us both

Before excuse me is this seat taken,
before the color of your eyes, before can I get you a drink,
before I'm Rico I'm Dita, before the fleeting touch
of a hand on a shoulder, it passed through us both
like a door opening a crack in your sleep.

Albert in the night

On the roof her shadow, a slow shadow,
a shadow that is gradually leaving me.
Indoors it is bad. Outside
it is dark. The bedroom at night
feels lower.

Butterflies to a tortoise

At sixteen and a half, in a country town, she was married to a well-off relative.
A widower aged thirty. It was the custom
to marry daughters within the family. Her father
was a gold and silver smith. One of the brothers was sent to Sofia,
to study to be a pharmacist and bring back a diploma. Nadia herself
learned from her mother how to cook and embroider,
make sweetmeats and write neatly. The widowed bridegroom, a draper,
came to visit on Sabbaths and holidays. If asked, he sang wonderfully
in a rich, resonant tenor voice. He was a tall, elegant, well-mannered man,
who always knew what to say
and what to pass over in silence. Nadia's heart
was not in the marriage, because her best friend whispered to her
what love was really like: it must not be stirred until it pleases.

But her parents, patiently, understandingly, brought her to another point
of view. Surely to do her duty was also in her own best interest. And they set
a date, not too soon; they wanted to give her enough time
to become accustomed gradually to the widower, who never failed
to bring her a present. Sabbath by Sabbath
she learned to like the sound of his voice. Which was pleasant.

After the wedding her husband turned out to be a considerate man
who inclined to a measure of regularity in intimate matters. Every evening,
scrubbed, scented and cheerful, he would come and sit on the edge
of the bed. He started with a gentle word of affection, turned out the light
to spare her blushes, drew aside the sheet, caressed her sparingly,
and eventually rested his hand on her breast. She was always

on her back, her nightdress rolled up, he was always on top of her,
while outside the door the pendulum wall-clock with gilt fittings
slowly beat time. He rammed. He groaned. Had she wished, every night
she could have counted about twenty moderate thrusts, the final one
reinforced with a tenor note. Then he wrapped himself up and slept.
In the thick darkness she lay empty and bewildered
for another hour at least. Sometimes solacing her body herself. In a whisper
she told her closest friend, who would say, When there is love
it feels different, but how can you explain butterflies to a tortoise.

Several times she woke at five, put on a housecoat and went up on the roof
to fetch in the washing. She could see empty rooftops, a patch of forest,
a deserted plain. Then her father and her husband, setting off together
to early-morning prayers. Day after day she shopped and cleaned
and cooked. On Sabbath eves guests came, imbibed and dined
and nibbled and argued. On her back in bed when it was all over
she sometimes had thoughts about a baby.

The story goes like this

After about three years it became clear that she could not give him children either. The widower, sadly, divorced her and married her cousin instead. Because of the shame and grief she was suffering her parents gave her permission to join her brother and sister-in-law who had settled in Israel, and live there under their supervision. Her brother rented a room for her on the roof of a building in Bat Yam and arranged for her to work in a sewing shop. The money she had received from the divorce he deposited in a savings account for her. And so, at the age of twenty, she was a single girl again. She enjoyed being on her own for much of the time. Her brother and his wife kept an eye on her, but in fact it was unnecessary. Sometimes she baby-sat for them in the evening and sometimes she went out with somebody or other to a café or the cinema, without getting involved. She was not attracted by the thought of being put on her back again with her nightdress rolled up; and she could easily keep her own body quiet. At work she was considered a serious, responsible worker and in general a lovely girl. One night she happened to go to the cinema with a quiet, sensible young man, an accountant who was distantly related to her sister-in-law. When he escorted her home he apologized for not flirting with her; it wasn't because he didn't find her attractive, heaven forbid, but, on the contrary, because he didn't know how to go about it. In the past some girls had made fun of him for this, he explained, and he even laughed at himself a little, but it was the plain truth. When he said this, she suddenly felt a sort of pleasant inner roughness at the nape of her neck in the roots of her hair that radiated warmth towards her shoulders and armpits, which is why she suggested, Let's meet again on Tuesday at eight o'clock. Almost joyfully Albert said: I'd like that.

The miracle of the loaves and the fishes

There was also sex for money. It happened in a low-roofed
backpackers' hostel in Kathmandu. She had a dark voice like a muffled bell,
not unlike a fado-singer's bitter wistfulness. She was a tall,
well-rounded woman from Portugal who had been thrown out of a convent
on account of temptation (which she had both committed and succumbed to).
The Saviour had forgiven her. Her trespasses were themselves
her penance and her penitence. Now she took in wayfarers for a modest
charge. Her name was Maria. She spoke some English. She was not young,
her makeup was thick, but her knees were shapely and her breasts
unrestrained. In the tender furrow that crossed the neckline of her dress
a pendant hung, two fine silver lines running down till they met at a cross
that appeared and disappeared and reappeared
at the opening of her dress whenever she moved or laughed or bent over.
The L-shaped room contained only some mattresses, a low cupboard,
a washbasin, an earthenware jug, some tin mugs. The four Dutchmen,
Thomas, Johan, Wim and Paul, drank a strange, sluggish beer
brewed locally from a mountain shrub known as monkey marrow. Rico
sipped it curiously: it was tepid, thick and rather bitter.

For a modest fee she would grant them "grace and favor" in her room. One
at a time, twenty minutes each. Or else all five of them at once,
at a discount. She had a weakness for really young, woman-hungry men
coming down off the mountains: they always gave her such a soft,
maternal feeling. For all she cared they could see her at work. Let them
watch, it would be more exciting. For them and for her. She guessed
at the pent-up rivers of desire accumulated by mountain climbers
up there, in the empty snowfields and stark valleys. There were five of them

and she was a woman, and their desperation
made her feel compassionate too. Now you, come close and just touch me
here, then back off. Now you. Now wait. Watch.

She took off her dress slowly, swaying her hips, her eyes lowered, as though
to some sacred chant inaudible to them. The little green cross
hanging on her chest quivered on its silver thread, caressed by her breasts.
Paul snickered. At once she covered up with both hands: no.
This would not do. She insisted: no laughing. Anyone who had come here
to mock could have his money back and go elsewhere. Here
everything was decent and unsullied; there was room for aching bodies
but not for filthy minds. This evening she had a yen for a wedding night:
she would bestow her favors on every groom, then lull them to sleep
on her belly, a she-wolf with her cubs. Just as the Christ
gave His body and His blood—
so she went on, until Thomas and Johan, on either side, sealed her lips.

Rico was last, feeling for her warm soft conch and missing. Her hands
slid down and guided him. He lingered inside for an eternity,
holding back, not thrusting, mastering the surge lest it end
like a fleeting dream. Wherefore the woman Maria was filled with tenderness
as waters cover the sea. As though seized with labor pains,
she clenched him lightly, with descending and ascending contractions:
suckling him and being suckled to the very last.

Back in Bat Yam his father upbraids him

Rebellious son. Stubborn son. I am asleep
but my heart is awake. My heart is awake
and makes lament,
the smell of my son is like the smell
of a harlot.
There is no peace for my bones
on account of your wanderings.
How long?

But his mother defends him

His mother says:
My view is different.
Wandering is fitting
for those who have lost their way.
Kiss the feet my son
of the woman Maria
whose womb, for an instant,
returned you to mine.

Bettine breaks

—But what more is going to happen between you and me, Albert? Here
we are again on your balcony in the evening. Under the neon light. It's not
you and another woman, it's not me and another man,
and it's not two other people either.
Herbal tea. Watermelon. Cheese. It's very nice of you
to buy me a present. A silk square. Can you really see me wearing
a thing like this? Round my neck? On my head? I've bought you a present too,
it's a scarf. Look: it's pure, soft Welsh wool. Good for the winter. Blue.
Checks. You sit facing me with your legs crossed, talking good sense
about Rabin and Peres. But you never mention her. Heaven forbid. So no one
gets upset.

But who will get upset if you do speak for once, Albert?
Are you worried you'll upset me? Or her? Or yourself? After all, we are
what we are, we're not partners and we're not family. We're not playing
the male-female game. You're sixty and I'm sixty. We're not a couple,
we're just two people. Acquaintances? Friends? Colleagues even? In a way?
An alliance for a rainy day? Twilight affection? Our legs crossed. Mine crossed
over mine, yours crossed over yours. You facing me and me facing you.
I read once that a man and a woman can't be just friends:
either they are lovers, or there is nothing between them. The fact is
I am just as bad as you. I don't say a word about Avram. I'm scared
that if I do talk about him you'll be so embarrassed
you'll run away again.

What is left? Herbal tea. Watermelon. Cheese. Investments.
Indexation. Savings accounts. Funds. Legs crossed, you

and I. Your leg over yours, mine over mine. Careful
with words in case we touch. I'm relaxed
and you are calm. The neon light casts a brightness
on all this. Below the veranda the gravel is dusty.
Forgive me Albert, don't be upset, I suddenly feel
like breaking a glass. There, that's done. I'm
sorry. You will forgive me. I'll sweep it up.
You needn't bother.

In the Temple of the Echo

A letter from Rico to Dita Inbar. Dear Dita, Kathmandu here, and this
is the scene. Going from one temple to another. Mainly out in the country.
I sometimes remember that thing we have, where I'm a nun
and you're a monk. If you can't remember, try. Though there's something
in Tel Aviv that rubs out memories. It's not the heat or the humidity.
Something else. Something more fundamental. Tel Aviv is a place
that rubs things out. Writing, rubbing out, while all the time we're breathing
chalk dust. Don't wait for me. Have some fun. Find yourself someone
who understands you, someone who's tough on the outside and soft
on the inside, sly in back and refined in front,
who advances on the left while forging ahead on the right, and go
if you can for a building contractor who'll let me live
in the gamekeeper's cottage. Don't get mad I'm only trying to say
that here in Tibet you really do remember things. Yesterday, for instance,
in the Temple of the Echo (so called because of an acoustic distortion
that turns a word into a wail, a shout into a laugh), I said your name twice
and you answered me from an underground cistern. Not you actually,
but a voice that was partly yours and partly my mother's. Don't worry.
I'm not mixing you up. She is herself and you are yourself. Take care
of yourself and don't go jumping into any empty swimming pools.
PS If you get a chance, look in on my dad and see how he's getting on.
I don't suppose he's complaining and I'm not either. The light here
is quite pleasant on the eyes, when it doesn't dazzle you.

Blessed

The light is sweet on the eyes. The darkness sees into the heart. The rope
follows the pail. The pitcher was broken at the fountain. The humble settler
who has never settled himself in the seat of the scornful will die in August
of cancer of the pancreas. The policeman who cried wolf will die
in September of heart failure. His eyes were sweet and the light is sweet
but his eyes are no more and the light is still here. The seat of the scornful
has been closed down, and in its place they've opened a shopping mall.
The scornful have passed away. Diabetes. Kidney disease. Blessed
is the fountain. Blessed is the pail. Blessed are the poor in spirit for
they shall inherit the wolf.

Missing Rico

At 7 p.m. in Café Limor with one Dubi Dombrov, a divorced lad
in his forties. He has a habit of panting like a thirsty dog, fast and hard,
through his mouth. His ginger hair is thinning but his bushy sideburns go
exactly halfway down his cheeks. Like a pair of brackets, she thinks, eyeing
his legs as he comes in and sits down, not facing her but by her side,
his thigh almost touching hers. The purpose of the meeting is to talk about
the film. This Dombrov is the number one man in a production company
that does some work with Channel 2, or hopefully soon will. He definitely
doesn't rule out the idea of doing something different, for a change.
Something experimental, like the screenplay Dita has written
and shown him. The only condition is that Dita should find
shall we say four thousand, give or take, and of course Dita herself must take
the part of Nirit. The fact is that while he was reading the script this Nirit
teased the pants off him. In bed at night it's her, only her, that he undresses.
Wet dreams, that's what you've given me, you or Nirit. Cross your heart:
is Nirit you?
And let's be quite clear that I'm serious and I and you and I and I.
He leers lecherously at her breasts—into her mouth he forces
a spoonful of ice-cream and pushes her hand between his legs, so she can
feel for herself what a hard-on she's given him. As big as a donkey's.
Dita pulls her hand away and leaves.

Back in her bedroom alone she unzips her skirt, in front of the mirror
she strips. She looks at her body: it's wild, it's new, it turns men on
and it turns her on too. This body wants sex and it wants it
now, this body wants Rico, it does, but how: Rico's not here.
She's got the itch, her body's in charge and she can't resist. Naked

she throws herself down on her bed, into her pillow she buries
her head then rolls herself over as quick as she can and hugs that pillow
as though it's her man. She wants to stop but her body says no, it's started
now and it's got to go. She ruffles and tickles his body fur so he'll have
gooseflesh just like her. She buries her face between his thighs and her tongue
plies wildly as her body sighs and she drips with juices like rare perfume
as her body is pierced by a tender tune. Their hands intertwine and she stifles
a groan. He is inside her but she's alone. When it's done, she plants six
little kisses in the soft of her arm for the man she misses, and then as she falls
asleep on her bed she counts to herself inside her head how much cash she has
stashed away and how can she raise the 4k to make a movie out of the script
that she wrote about the love of Nirit. Cross your heart: is Nirit you?
That's a question Dita's not got an answer to.

No butterflies and no tortoise

The forecast, that had promised a chance of snow on high ground,
had not kept its promise. But Nadia, who had promised nothing, appeared
at his door one Saturday morning, in a light-colored frock
with a red scarf round her neck, somewhere between a girl and a woman. Did I
surprise you? Are you free? (Am I free? Oh, painfully free. His heart dissolved
in bashful glee. Nadia. Has come. To visit. Me.)
Albert was renting a room from a childless couple in old Bat Yam. They were
away for the weekend. The flat was all his. He sat Nadia down on his bed
and went to the kitchen to slice some black bread, and came back bearing
a tray with a choice of feta or honey. He paced round the room,
then returned to the kitchen, and chopped some tomatoes to make
a salad so fine and well-seasoned, as though this would convince her
that he was right. He would not let her lift a finger to help him. He made
an omelette. Put the kettle on. Like a man in his element. This surprised her,
because previously whenever they went out together to a café or the cinema
Albert had seemed so hesitant and unassertive. And now it emerged
that at home he did precisely what he wanted, and what he wanted was to do
everything himself. She touched his hand with her fingertip:
thank you. It's nice here.

Coffee. Biscuits. But how do you start on love on a rainy Saturday morning
like this, in a shabby room in old Bat Yam in the mid-Sixties?
(In the headlines in the paper on the kitchen table Nasser threatened
and Eshkol warned of the risk of escalation.) The light flickered. The room
was small. Nadia sat. Albert faced her. Neither of them knew how to begin.

The would-be lover was a shy young man, who had only ever dreamed
of sleeping with a woman. He dreaded yet wanted it; he wanted it
but was deterred by a faint fear of bodily embarrassments.
His would-be partner, a reserved divorcee, lived in a room on a roof,
sewed for a living, her past was somewhat conventional. She
was no hind and he was no young hart. How and with what
do you begin to love? Nadia sat. Albert stood.

Outside it was raining again, the rain getting heavier, teeming down on rows
of dull grey shutters along the empty wet street; hammering on overturned
dustbins, polishing the panes in the tight-shut windows, pouring down
on rooftops, on forests of antennae trembling in the freezing wind that beat
on zinc tubs hanging on grilles of kitchen balconies. And the gutters
grunted and choked like an old man sleeping fitfully. How do you start
love now? Nadia stood. Albert sat.

Through the wall from the next-door flat came the Saturday morning
program on the radio. A musical quiz. Nadia is here but where am I?
He tried to tell her some news from the office, not to break the thread
of the conversation. But the thread was no thread. She was waiting
and he was waiting for whatever would come at the end of the thread.
What would come? And who would make it come? She was embarrassed.
So was he. He kept on and on trying to explain something in economics.
Instead of words like credit side, debit side, Nadia heard, My sister,
my bride. And when he spoke of bulls and bears she translated, You have
doves' eyes. While he was talking she reached for a cushion, and Albert
trembled because on the way the warmth of her breast touched his back.

It's up to me to overcome his fear. What would a really experienced woman
do now in my place? She cut in: apparently, all of a sudden, she had a speck
of dust in her eye. Or a fly. He bent over to get a good look. Now his face
was close to her brow, she could clasp his temples with her hands, and at last
lower his lips for a pleasing, teasing first kiss.

Two weeks later, in her room on the roof, between two rainshowers, he asked
for her hand. He did not say, Be my wife, but instead: If you'll marry me
then I'll marry you. Because it was Nadia's second marriage they had a small,
intimate party, at her brother and sister-in-law's home, with a handful
of relatives and a few friends, and the elderly couple in whose flat
Albert lodged. After the ceremony and the party they took a taxi
to the Sharon Hotel. Albert undid the straining hooks one by one
down the back of her wedding dress. Then the bride turned out the light
and they both undressed modestly, in total darkness, on opposite sides
of the bed. They groped their way toward each other. She sensed
she would have to teach him: after all I presumably know
better than he does. It turned out however that shy Albert could teach her
something she neither knew nor imagined: the broad, flowing surge of joy
of one who was shy as long as the light was on but in the pitch dark
was insatiable. In the dark he entered into his own element.
No butterflies now and no tortoise at all, but like a hart panting for water
or a swallow for its nest. His chest to her back, and belly to belly, horse
and his rider and into every breach.

And what is hiding behind the story?

The fictional Narrator puts the cap back on his pen and pushes away the
writing pad. He is tired. And his back aches. He asks himself how on earth
he came to write such a story. Bulgarian, Bat Yam, written in verse
and even, here and there, in rhyme. Now that his children have grown up
and he has known the joy of grandchildren, and he has produced
several books and traveled and lectured and been photographed, why should
he suddenly return to versification? As in the bad old days of his youth
when he used to run away at night to be all alone in the reading room
on the edge of the kibbutz where he would cover page after page with jackals'
howls. An acne-scarred, yellow-haired, angular boy forever swallowing insults,
with his high-falutin talk arousing some ridicule and some pity, hanging
around the girls' quarters, hoping that Gila or Tsila might want him
to read them a poem he had just written. Naively imagining that a woman
is acquired by a sermon or a verse. And indeed he sometimes managed to stir
something inside those girls that later, in the night, accompanied them
when they went to the woods to give and receive love, not with him but with
burly haymakers who reaped with joy what he had sown with his words
almost in tears. He is almost sixty, this Narrator, and he might sum it up
roughly as follows: there is love and there is love. In the end everyone is left
alone: those hairy haymakers, and Tsila, and Gila, and Bettine, and Albert,
and even the Narrator in question. And he who is climbing mountains
in Tibet and she who embroidered in the quiet of her bedroom. We go and
we come, we see and we want until it is time to shut up and leave. And then
silence. Born in Jerusalem lives in Arad looked around him and wanted this
and that. Since he was a child he has heard, impatiently, time and again
from Auntie Sonya, a woman who suffers, that we should be happy with
what we have. We should always count our blessings. Now he finds himself

at last quite close to this way of thinking. Whatever is here, the moon and the breeze, the glass of wine, the pen, words, a fan, the desk lamp, Schubert in the background, and the desk itself: a carpenter who died nine years ago worked hard to make you this desk so that you would remember that you didn't start from nothing. From starlight down to olives, or soap, from a thread to a shoelace, from a sheet to the autumn. It wouldn't be a bad thing to leave behind in return a few lines worthy of the name. All this is diminishing. Disintegrating. Fading. What has been is being gradually wrapped in pallor. Nadia and Rico, Dita, Albert, Stavros Evangelides the Greek who brought up the dead and then died himself. The Tibetan mountains will last for a while, as will the nights, and the sea. All the rivers flow into the sea, and the sea is silence silence silence. It's ten o'clock. Dogs are barking. Take up your pen and return to Bat Yam.

Refuge

Dita is at the door. On her slender back a mountain of a backpack
with another bundle tied to it, clutching some plastic bags
and a handbag: she is seeking refuge, for a couple of days,
a week at most, if it's not an imposition. She's ended up with no flat
and no money, all her savings and everything gone; she found
some kind of producer, got taken for a ride. But why are you standing
in the doorway? You'll fall over. Come inside. Then you can
tell me all about it. We'll have a think. We'll get you out of this mess.

She gulped down a soft drink. Undressed. Took a shower. For a moment
she embarrassed him when she emerged wrapped in a towel from mid-breast
to thigh. She stood in front of him
in the kitchen and told him in detail how she had got stung.
And her parents were abroad and their flat was let, she had simply nowhere
to turn. It was no good his staring down at the floor:
the sight of her naked feet
sets his heart at odds with his body.

Rico's room is yours from now on. It's empty
anyway. Here is the bedding. That's the air-conditioning. His wardrobe isn't
too tidy, but there's some room. I'll bring you a cold drink in a minute.
Lie down. Get some rest. We'll talk later. If you need me for anything
just say Albert and I'll be right there. Don't be shy. Or simply come
to my office. It's through there. I'll just be sitting finishing off some accounts.
You're no trouble at all. On the contrary: for some time now—
He stopped himself. Under the towel her hips made a whispering sound
and he was blushing as though he had been caught red-handed.

In the light-groping darkness

A widowed father with an honest name
lies wide awake in the night consumed with shame:
a sleeping woman the cause of his pain.

She's there alone—his eyes are open wide—
next door she's lying naked, on her side.
So young. A child. My daughter, my bride!

He switches on the bedside light and blinks
at his son and wife on the sideboard. He thinks
for a while. Then pads to the kitchen and drinks.

He sits down at his desk and begins to dream
heavy thoughts: his shadow stares back from the screen.
What a difficult summer, he types, this has been.

From the garden outside where nothing has stirred
in the light-groping darkness, a single bird:
narimi narimi. Yes, I heard.

Restless he stands: how he longs to spread
a blanket on her, and stroke her head.
He stifles these feelings, and goes back to bed.

He turns and tosses. Of sleep there's no sign.
He turns on the light and checks the time:
it's five o'clock here—so in Tibet it's nine.

In lieu of prayer

It's nine in the morning now in Bhutan. Without the Dutchmen. On a bench
in a wood the youth sits wrapped in a blanket, absorbing
the mountain shadows among the mountains. A tranquil silence
envelops the view. How empty and strange the light here flows, light
longing for shade. Light shading itself. Wind in the grass. A deserted valley.
True peace shall surely come.

The woman Maria

remembers him: the last of the boys.
His brow. His eyes. The groan as he came.
The touch of his arm and the spring of his seed. When the others had left
he came back and kissed the soles of her feet.

A feather

After four troubled nights he went back to Bostros Street for a second visit
to the old Greek who called forth the dead. True, on his previous visit
all that his money had bought him was two glasses of water, one lukewarm
and the other cool and fresh. And a picture of a crucified Christ-child
looking as though the Crucifixion and the Resurrection had preceded
the raising of Lazarus and the other miracles. As he left he had seen a woman
going down the street who had looked a little like her from behind. This time
he would not give up. He would follow her to the ends of

Mr. Stavros Evangelides, the eighty-year-old sorcerer, his bald head patterned
with brown stains, moles and sparse grey bristles, his Phoenician nose,
big and protruding, but his teeth were young, and his joyful, guileless
eyes, which seem to see only good, looked down at the visitor
from a sepia photograph in a tortoiseshell frame. In his place was a skinny
crow-like old woman with cracked leathery skin and an evil mouth. She
motioned him to sit, claimed her fee, counted the cash, went out, returned,
and handed him a glass containing a viscous liquid with a yellow taste.
While he drank she bent over him. Sweet and terrible the smell of her flesh
hit him, a smell of decay. She waited. Motionless. Her dress was embroidered.
Once or twice her beak opened wide, parched with thirst, closed then opened
a crack. *Narimi,* she cried harshly and flew away. In his bosom
one black feather remained.

Nirit's love

Dubi Dombrov Productions Ltd. woke up at ten o'clock, sweaty and
thick-headed. He went for a piss, his eyelids still gummed together, then
turned on the tap and washed in cold water. He thought about shaving.
Couldn't be bothered. Put on a rancid shirt from yesterday, and clumsily
groped his way to the kitchen to make some coffee. When he went
to the rack for a clean cup a spider ran away. Why? What's the matter?
What have I done? I'd never harm you, so why are you running away from me?
Barefoot, tired, he sat down to wait for the water to boil and remembered
Nirit's Love, that script by Dita Inbar. And the money. True, it wasn't exactly
honest what I did, but she had only herself to blame, and why did she have to
show me, right to my face, that she found me disgusting, like some lower kind
of scum? Surely even a repulsive man has a right to be attracted to
a woman, has a right to finer feelings which a woman can choose to
ignore, but why must she rub salt in the wound? Why did she have to
show me how disgusted she was? And just when I was thinking that she
was different from all the rest, that she had a higher tolerance.
My fatal mistake was that like an idiot apparently I identified her
with her screenplay, where this Nirit takes pity on a real dog of a man. As for
the money, no one has ever given anything back to me. Everyone has always
taken from me. All I've ever had back has been insults.

A Psalm of David

In a hanged man's house one must not mention that the rope follows
the pail. It is not in vain that a woman is bewitched by a nocturnal shade,
and gives her body to a wandering minstrel in Adullam, or here on the plains
of Bhutan. At your age David of the beautiful eyes did not play the harp,
only with his reed pipe did he make the hinds to dance. And this was the
instrument that drew Michal and Ahinoam and the woman of Carmel to him
like a rope. Such a plain, homely instrument, but maidens were beguiled by
its strange, mournful sound, the ruddy-faced rascal who leaped and danced
and grazed his flocks among the lilies, chasing the wind and deflowering
women whose storm-racked flesh bristled under his hand that was soaked in
the fat of the mighty and their blood, skilled with the sling. So he roamed,
slew, loved, smote his tens of thousands, and so he became king. After many
years, on that great oak tree, the rope followed the pail.
Then came mourning. The house of a hanged man. Then came the harp
of the psalms. Finally came the dagger. How the day has faded. Passed.
Now all is dust.

David according to Dita

How the day has faded. When were we talking about King David,
how did we get to talking about him? Do you remember, Dita? One Friday
night at Giggy Ben-Gal's in Melchett Street. You dragged me out of the party
onto the balcony and at the window opposite a beefy man wearing nothing
but an undershirt and his loneliness was polishing his glasses
against the light, he put them on, saw us watching and shut
his shutters. And then because of him you told me what it is
about a man that attracts you: the Charles Aznavour type, or Yevgeny
Yevtushenko. From them you went on to King David. It attracts
you when there is a needy side, a rascally side and a side
that plays the fool. And you also showed me from the balcony that night
what a ragged sexy city this Tel Aviv is.
You don't see a sunset or a star, you see how the plaster
peels from an excess of adrenaline smells of sweat and diesel fuel a tired
city that doesn't want to sleep at the end of the day it wants to go out wants it
to happen wants it to end and then wants more. But David, you said,
reigned for thirty years in Jerusalem the ultra-Orthodox City of David
which he could not stand and which could not stand him
with his leaping and dancing and his one-night stands.
It would have been more fitting for him to reign in Tel Aviv,
to roam the city like a General (Retd.) who is both a grieving parent
and a well-known philanderer, a loaded high-liver and a king
who composes music and writes poetry and sometimes gives a recital,
"The Sweet Psalmist," in a trendy venue then goes
off to the pub to drink with young fans and groupies.

She comes to him but he is busy

She has made him some tea and brought him some crackers and olives
and goat cheese on a tray and now here she is barefoot in the doorway
of his room, feeling partly like a daughter and partly like a waitress,
waiting for him to turn his tired head. But he has not noticed. He
is hunched over a document, absorbed in checking the details
of the rotten agreement she has so incautiously signed. She has been
taken for a ride. She had such high hopes. He finds that all she gets
in return for the money is not a commitment but, at best, only
a conditional intent. It is a contemptible contract, yet so full of holes
that even without lawyers there is a fair chance of rescuing her
and putting pressure on him to pay back the money.

Barefoot with her tray she waits for him to notice her. If she calls him
he will start and his voice will tremble. Yesterday evening she said Albert
and he jumped, almost shuddered. What will happen if she touches
his hand, not like a woman but like a child asking
When are you going to stop being busy?

He glances at his watch: ten to five. Ten to nine out in Nepal. He'll
pay it back, and how: we'll scare him. At the meeting
tomorrow we'll point out, here and here, how we'll nail him if he tries
to get clever. On the other hand, if he admits his errors and makes amends,
our side may consider taking no further action on this occasion.

While he is still making notes, the tray arrives with the touch of her hand,
not like a daughter but like a bold schoolgirl, deliberately
teasing a middle-aged teacher who is shy but endearing.

He isn't lost and even if he is

Crystalline silence, transparent and blue.
The wind has died. Over deserted plains
a veil of glassy frost descends.

Cold and empty. Vast. Just over the horizon
according to the map there is a little village.
There is no sign of the village. Perhaps he is lost.

He will press on a little further. If he is lost
never mind: he will give up and go back
silently. The way he came.

The road is level. The frost is fine and bright.
Beside the sea his father is waiting
and beyond, in the depths, his mother.

Desire

His father is waiting and so is his mother and Dita is with them
in a strange shack and the woman Maria and the mountain shadows
and the roar of the sea and David and Michal and Jonathan too,
and there is no limit to their passionate longing many waters cannot quench
and mighty rivers cannot drown. See, he is returning to them filled.

Like a miser who has sniffed a rumor of gold

But what is the Narrator trying to say? Is he resentful? Is his blood pounding
or his heart aching or his flesh bristling on the threshold? Here he has made
a list of words: in the word woods there is a vague dread. In the word hills is
a world of lust. If you say shack, or meadow, or wayfarer, rain, compassion,
at once he lights up like a miser who has sniffed a rumor of gold. Or if,
for instance, the evening paper prints the phrase "new horizons," at once
I am on my way to bathe twice in the same river.

Shame

A miser who has sniffed a rumor of gold should wrap himself in dark robes.
Mr. Danon is working as usual compiling balance sheets on his computer
screen. Next screen previous screen. Checking every entry. His heart is not
in it. In vain he clears his mind, he has no refuge from her smell. Her smell
on her towel her smell on her sheets whom did she call whom did she talk to.
Her smell in the kitchen where has she gone where has she gone when
will she be back in the hall her smell in the living room her smell who
has she gone out with what is there between them. Her smell in the bathroom
where has she gone and what if she is taken for a ride again. The smell
of her shampoo. Her smell in the laundry basket. Where has she gone. When
will she be back. She'll be back late. In the Himalayas it's already tomorrow.
Where can I hide from her smell.

He lies in the dark with his life in his hands. Her breasts are so soft, her juice
running over the down of her thighs but he is alone. With half of his pleasure
still warm in his hand he shuffles to the washbasin, shattered. A man
of his age. His son's girlfriend. He should wrap himself in dark robes
but where can he take his disgrace. Tomorrow night he should get out of here
and seek sleep in some hotel. Perhaps Bettine would take him in?

He resembles

It would be interesting to know what she is thinking about now, what is the source of that secret smile, like a drowsy, satisfied cat. She is remembering a morning of love in a hotel in Eilat in the springtime. She didn't feel like a swim and she didn't feel like getting up. They stayed in bed with the air-conditioning on, sated with night games, she in half a bikini and he stark naked, their skin still pink and hot from the beach yesterday. Breakfast in bed and a game of rummy, laughing at nothing at all, looking for a rhyme for stowaway. Throw-away. Go away. I stow away, you stowed away, he has stown away. Then, with pencil and paper, listing palindromes. Collapsing with laughter at this too. Noon. Boob. Poop. Toot. (As in, toot if you've pooped.) Whoever found a new word could demand a forfeit. In the course of this game Dita discovered some-thing she had never noticed before, that Rico could write with either hand. I've never seen anything like that before; let's see now if you can write with your toes. He tried and scribbled and made her laugh. He explained that he was not born ambidextrous, he was actually born left-handed, but his parents made him write with his right hand and even punished him if he didn't. Especially his mother, because where she came from left-handedness was considered a handi-cap, a sign of poor upbringing, the mark of a bad family background. They forced me to be right-handed, and the result is that now I can write with either.

She took them both and placed them here and here, let's see which of them is more left-handed. They ended up playing at deflowering the virgin and seduc-ing the monk, until they fell asleep. Later they showered and went down, fam-ished, to look for a fish restaurant. In the evening they went for a swim. Now, remembering, she wanted him. She went to a film with Giggy Ben-Gal and they ate in a pub, and then went back to his place. When she got back it was nearly one o'clock, but she found the old man waiting up for her. Was he worried?

Was he jealous? He made her a snack which she didn't eat because she wasn't hungry. But she sat in the kitchen with him for half an hour and he told her something about how drab life was in those days and even a little, in passing, about Rico's mother. Finally, filled with nocturnal courage, he revealed to her that he had a girlfriend, not exactly a girlfriend, a lady friend, who worked in the Property Tax Board, not a lady friend either really but an undefined sort of relationship. Dita was curious to know whether he had touched his "undefined relationship" yet, but she didn't feel she could ask. Interesting, why did he tell me? It came out as though he was writing a word, rubbing it out, and writing another one on top of it, and that reminded her of his son. And his way of putting his hand between his collar and his neck sometimes for no reason at all, or explaining things as though he were threading beads. Is he left-handed too, but still in the closet? Such a sensitive man. So sweet. I wonder when he ever sleeps.

The Narrator copies from the dictionary of idioms

One who has come through fire and water, his early promise
has come to nothing. It has not come easily to him. He has come to blows.
He has not come up in the world nor has he come into money.
He has come to grief, has come down to his last crust. Now
he has come to judgment, and at last he
has come to terms.

A postcard from Thimphu

Dear Dad and Dita. We were cut off yesterday while we were talking. I didn't
manage to tell you how pleased I am the two of you are together at home.
It's good that you're not alone either of you. It's a good solution for you both.
You look after her and you look after him, etc. Cooking and eating
and washing up and taking turns emptying the rubbish. I like this
father-daughter couple thing, this two-track relationship, as if you've gained
a daughter Dad and Mother and I have gained a double. Dad, I expect
you're the one who puts both your laundry in the machine, not sorting it
into his and hers but only into cotton and synthetics. And Dita, I imagine
you're the one who does the shopping for both of you and Dad you make
one of your salads, no mortal hand can chop vegetables finer than you. So
you've ended up with no money and no flat Dita, well Dad, you'll sort
that out for her. And as Mother used to say, every cloud has a silver lining,
and in this case the lining is also fun. Dita I can almost see you sleeping in
my bed, where Dad you come in every night as usual to cover her up, but
Dita you push and kick the covers off again. An anarchist in your sleep.
The opposite of Mother, who even on summer nights wrapped herself up
like a mummy. She wore a blue nightie trimmed with lace. You ought to
ask him if you can wear it one night. You won't refuse her, will you?
It's on the top shelf of the wardrobe, on the left. The little that Mother needs
now she can find with me: she, who could never stand long journeys, who
could never sleep in a strange bed, comes all the way here sometimes,
and naturally I don't tell her to go away.

A pig in a poke

A repulsive fellow with sweaty armpits, he is forty minutes late, he apologizes, Bat Yam is like Bombay to him, his brain's dehydrated before he found it, and on top of everything else he's parked illegally. He is oozing good will and wants to settle the whole business in good faith, and even, let's say, make a fresh start. When all is said and done, it's nothing more than a little misunderstanding: he will only use her money if and when there is a production, otherwise he'll return every last shekel (after deduction of expenses, etc.). What a pity she's not in: he was hoping to explain to her personally that bygones are bygones, his intentions were definitely honorable. Mr. Danon spoke sternly: the contract was crooked, and not entirely aboveboard from the tax point of view either. As he spoke the producer sat before him, worn-out, sweat-soaked and unkempt, a shamefaced, heavily panting dog, in his forties, his thinning red hair offset by Hapsburg sideburns going down to the angle of his jaw, a woebegone creature whom no woman except his mother had ever touched without an ulterior motive. Mr. Danon fetched a bottle of mineral water and poured a glass and then refilled it. While the producer was drinking as though he was dying of thirst, Mr. Danon pondered the expression benefit in kind, which contains a hint of corruption but also a touch of desperation. Likewise the word crafty.

Mr. Danon spoke in a tone of polite reprimand, like a pedantic father. The producer listened with his head to one side and his mouth wide open, as though his sense of hearing were located in his throat rather than his ears. At least three times he insisted that he was really an honest man and that Dombrov was a respectable company and that he was sorry to have given the impression. There and then he signed an agreement to return the money in full in two equal installments. Let's say there's a distinct possibility that the film will materialize; she's truly gifted and she's come up with a peach of a script, though not exactly what the market goes for these days. After signing he stayed on for half an hour or so and polished off another bottle of mineral water, talking about the state of the media, which is being ruined by commercialization, which in fact, let's be clear, is destroying everything here. Mr. Danon fetched another bottle, because Dombrov—call me Dubi—displayed a bottomless thirst. He insisted on being pleasant and inspiring confidence, prepared to debase himself so long as he made a good impression. He began to expand on an idea he had conceived about the eternal conflict between genuine art and popular taste. So he gained some more time in the company of his paternal host, who appeared to be sensible, attentive, just the way he himself would be happy to appear on the stage of life but had never managed to. And besides, on another matter, tax, for some years now I've had an accountant, Mr. So-and-So, from whom I have never had an ounce of human warmth. Is it out of the question, let's say, for me to put myself in your hands? Be looked after by you personally? That is to say as a client who needs an occasional guiding hand? Actually "guiding hand" might seem to be a religious expression, whereas I am, let's be clear, an ardent secularist, even though there are moments—but that's nothing at all to do with what we were talking about. I'm sorry, I've wandered off the point again. I need a guiding hand. Actually I've been like that ever since my wife left me for a well-known singer. And by the way my parents, both of them, were killed in the El Al disaster when I was a child. So that now, let's say at the present juncture in my life, I'm coming to terms the hard way with the fact that I'll probably never be the Israeli Steven Spielberg. A pig in a poke is an expression that generally denotes an unconsidered purchase, but in my case it describes my actual condition, both commercially and personally, or, let's say, existentially. But how did we get on to that? After all, we were only talking about the occasional tax advice and making up my annual accounts.

Mr. Danon apologized, he couldn't take on, overwhelmed with work, etc., but finally, on the doorstep, to their mutual surprise, he suddenly heard himself utter the words Call me, we'll talk about it.

She goes out and he stays in

At six she woke from a heavy siesta. She took a shower
and washed her hair. Stopped in the doorway of his room,
wearing only a wet shirt that did not quite cover her underwear.
I slept like a log and I must rush to work (receptionist
in a hotel). Be a dear and lend me two hundred shekels
just till the end of the week, will you. There's some rice and chicken
in the fridge and tonight after the news there's a program
about Tibet. Will you watch and tell me about it tomorrow?
She combed her hair, dressed and stopped in his doorway again,
I'm off now, bye, and don't you dare wait up for me,
just you go to bed, don't worry, I promise not to take any sweets
from strangers. She blew him a kiss and left him
changing a light bulb in the hall, in deepening gloom.

And when the shadows overwhelmed him

And if she stays out all night what will he do all night, and if she gets back
at midnight and goes straight to bed what will he do while she sleeps?
Tomorrow he'll tell her that her money is safe, that from now on
she is free and he is of no further use. Around nine there was a power outage,
and like a solitary mountaineer on whom night falls in a deserted place
he groped and found a flashlight and shifted the blocks of shadow around.
When the shadows overwhelmed him he gave up and went
to Bettine's, which was also in darkness with only an emergency light
glowing palely by her bed. And as the lights did not come back on
and the emergency light was fading he found himself telling her how
a bedraggled bird had nested uninvited in his flat, and how today he
himself had made sure—why on earth had he done it—that she too
would soon fly away. Reading between the lines, Bettine picked up
his secret and found it partly ridiculous and partly moving and painful. She
took his hand in hers, and they listened to the tossing and turning
of the sea in the depths of the dark, and then came a reaching out, a shy
embrace with no clothing removed, partly for loneliness of the flesh
and partly for grace and favor. Bettine knew from her flesh that he
was imagining another in her but she forgave him: had it not been
for the other, this would never have happened.

A shadow harem

Wisely, firmly, yet gently, he had rescued and retrieved
her lost cash. And what was the outcome? Simply
that in another day or two she would pluck her underwear
off the washing line, blow him a kiss, and vanish. The wrong
had been righted, but an invisible hand, not his own,
certainly not his right hand, possibly his left, had mockingly
frustrated him. Fear not. It was not in vain. With her going, the shade
of the dead one will surely return to be with you.
And hers too. The shades of two women. And Bettine as well.
A shadow harem under the shade of your roof.

Rico considers his father's defeat

Dad's sitting reading a paper. Dad's watching the news headlines.
His face is pained, like a disappointed teacher: reprimanding, chiding
the state of the world whose antics really go
too far. The time has come to take steps. He has
made up his mind to respond severely.

My father's severity is ineffectual. A poor man's severity. Weary fading
powerless. Instead there is a touch of sadness about him, an air of
resignation. He is not a young man. He's just a humble citizen.
What difference can he make
with his puny cane. And sometimes my father quotes the verse:
As the sparks fly upward, man is born unto labor. But what is he trying
to say to me? That I should fly upward? Or get a job? Not to fight
lost battles? My father's severity. His defeated shoulders.
Because of them I left. To them I shall return.

Rico reconsiders a text he has heard from his father

And there's another great text in Job that he quotes to me
so that I'll remember that property and possessions are
not the most important thing: Naked came I forth from my mother's womb
and naked shall I return thither. So what is the point of the race to amass
and hoard so-called belongings. My father is blind
to the hidden secret of this verse: her womb
is waiting for me. I came forth. I shall return. The cross on the way
is less important.

The cross on the way

He circles aimlessly around. And returns. Between one sleep and the next
he barely wakes. He travels from village to remote village. A day here a day
there. He meets Israelis, what's new back home, and falls asleep. He meets
women, exchanges a first signal and gives up. Like a tortoise.
On his travels he has crossed three or four maps. So what if he crosses
yet another, more valleys. Another climb. This view has run out.
His money too, almost. With a little luck he'll make it to Bangkok,
where the money his father sent is waiting. And then Sri Lanka. Or Rangoon.
In the autumn he'll go home. Or not. By a feeble light in a hostel, lying
neither sleeping nor waking, like an invalid waiting for it to become clear
one way or the other, seeing on the sooty ceiling stains of mountains
suspended between one shadow and the next. Not to climb but to find
a way in, or a way through, an opening, or a narrow crack, through which

Seabed bird

Shortly before my death a bird on a branch enticed me.
Narimi its feathery down touched me wrapped all of me
in a marine afterbirth.

Night after night, my widower weeps on his pillow, where has she gone
whom my soul loves. My orphan child is wandering far, conjuring omens.
Child bride you are their wife, you have my nightdress,
you have their love. My flesh is wasted. Set me as a seal.

He hesitates, nods and lays out

He returns from Bettine's when the power is restored and sits for a while
on the veranda alone. It is still August but the night is almost chilly, the cool
of the sea is an advance payment on the autumn. Around one o'clock,
five already in Bhutan, he drinks some chilled fruit juice
and goes to bed. Who knows who she is out on the town with
at this moment, she must be shivering in her light clothes. He gets up
and spreads a blanket on her bed and then hesitates,
nods and lays out on her pillow a blue nightdress,
because she is bound in her sleep to kick off the blanket.

Outsiders

Now for a riddle: what if anything does the shabby film producer Dubi
Dombrov have in common with the fictional Narrator who is about to
bring him back to Albert for a second visit? Besides the fact that both of them
require the services of a tax adviser, we may note some other parallels. He and I
as children were both outsiders. And we were both orphaned
at a fairly tender age and in need of a guiding hand, which is, as
Dubi observed, both an unquenchable personal need and, shall we say, a
religious quest. Both of us would like to create at least one work
that will turn out properly. And we are both on our way. True, he is a
clumsy, sloppy man, a thing of shreds and patches, which ostensibly
contrasts with the Narrator, who is well known to be a punctilious person
who always puts each thing away in its proper place. But that is only
on the outside. Inside him too there is an almighty mess.

And we are both always thirsty. Incidentally, a pig in a poke is an expression
that generally describes an incautious purchase but in our case connotes
not so much the impetuosity of the purchaser as the condition of the pig.
Sometimes we encounter a spider or a cockroach in the kitchen, which
we would never dream of hurting, but when the creature runs away from us
we take offence. And in general we are easily hurt:
we are constantly offended but contain ourselves, and continue to invite
further offence. With women he has a harder time of it: the Narrator
is apparently helped by a certain glow, at least on the surface. Like
the producer, he feels not entirely worthy, like a con man obtaining favors
by deception: be my mother, my sister, etc. Not to mention the fact that both
characters are a bit like David, who always longed to adopt a gentle brother
and a tough-warm father, a grim father whose manner toward his son implies

a suppressed rebuke. And yet, adopting a father, as can be seen
in the case of David, generally ends up in a battle in which the father's role
is to fall, thus restoring to us the liberties of orphanhood. And,
it may be added, both the unsuccessful producer and this Narrator
know the summer will soon be over.

Synopsis

To sum up the story so far, this is actually a tale about five or six characters, most of whom are alive most of the time, who often offer each other a hot or cold drink, generally a cold one, because it is summer. Sometimes they bring each other a tray with some cheese and olives, some wine, slices of watermelon, occasionally they even make each other a light meal. Or else you could see it as a number of intersecting triangles. Rico his father and his mother. Dita and her two lovers (Giggy Ben-Gal doesn't count). Albert between Bettine Carmel and his child bride who slips from room to room wearing no more than the shirt on her back. And Bettine herself, between Avram and Albert, her choice for a rainy day. While Dubi is stuck between his desire for Nirit and the rebuke of her warm-hearted representative on earth, to the love of women preferring the reproach of the sensible father. Rico, between his father and his cross, mistakenly searching in the mountains for his sea-tossed mother, in love with Dita though not loving her enough. Dita who is still waiting. And all of them are among shadows. Even the Narrator himself is somewhere between the mystical and the mischievous. This fabric resembles the pattern in the curtain at the Greek necromancer's, who died and left in his place a crow-woman. She has no living soul and her fabric gives a foretaste of the worm. And so a certain shadow falls over this story too.

The peace process

Hadhramaut. On his map such a principality appears in southern
Arabia, east of Bab el-Mandeb. Maybe the peace process
will open it up to us. But what is there there? Shifting sands,
wilderness, the haunt of foxes. But what is there here, in this abandoned
temple? A solitary Buddhist monk, a skeletal figure, through a hatch
wordlessly handing you a bowl of cold rice
and disappearing. He will not open the gate: you are not worthy yet.
In other words, the peace process is slow and painful. You will have
to make one or two further concessions. Only what is truly
a matter of life and death should not be negotiable.

In the middle of the hottest day in August

At Giggy Ben-Gal's, in Melchett Street. She is sleeping with him again
because she feels sorry for herself. While he saws away, she is thinking of
dear, good Albert, who worked so hard to find her
a one-room flat in Mazeh Street, the unfashionable side. On the
one hand it's good news, but on the other she really doesn't want
to move out. She enjoys living with him, he makes such a fuss of her
and his devotion is touching, not to mention his hungry look. All
the sweeter for being forbidden. This Giggy is a big brute. He fucks
as though he's hammering in nails or scoring points. One way
or another, in the end everyone is alone. In this heat
the best thing to be is a Buddhist nun in Tibet.

The riddle of the good carpenter who had a deep bass voice

In fact they were distantly related, both born in Sarajevo, Albert Danon from Bat Yam and my carpenter Elimelech who made this desk for me and died nine years ago. The great love of his life, apart from his wife and daughters, was opera: he had a stereo at home, another in his workshop, and a third in the car, hundreds of records and cassettes, dozens of performances. You could tell from two streets away if the workshop was open, not from the buzzing of the electric saw or the smell of sawdust and wood glue, but from the music: La Traviata, Don Giovanni, Rigoletto, the man was a total addict. We called him Shalyapin, because while he was planing away he would be roaring and booming, shamelessly out of tune, plunging so low as to put the deepest bass to shame. His voice was like the voice of the dead: a profundo *de profundis.* And yet this thunderous bass sound burst forth from a chest of modest dimensions, in fact Elimelech the carpenter was actually a slightly built man; his face was wrinkled with irony, one eyebrow was raised, and his glance contradicted itself: partly asking forgiveness and partly impish or sarcastic, as if to say, Who or what am I, but then you too, sir, excuse me for mentioning it, began as a drop of moisture and will end up as a broken vessel. The desk he made me, on which I am writing these words, turned out heavy. Massive. With no frills. A desk with the legs of a rhinoceros and sides like the shoulders of a market porter. A bass table. A proletarian object, thickset as a wrestler. Unlike Elimelech the carpenter, a man who loved to joke and tease but at the same time was being secretly, relentlessly eaten away by a ruthless canker, until one day he upped and hanged himself. He left no note, and no one could explain it. Least of all his wife and daughters. When I went to the hanged man's house to offer my condolences, I had the impression that grief had been displaced by surprise: as if all those years it had never occurred to them that here in their home an alien being was living among them in disguise, a maharajah masquerading as a wood-worker, and one day he had been summoned home, and at once, without a word, had shed his familiar disguise and set off for the place where he belonged. The last man, literally the last man in the world, to go and hang himself. For the life of us we wouldn't have dreamed that he had it in him. And there was no reason either: all things considered, life treated him very well, he had a family, friends, made a decent living, and he was the kind of man who was, as they say, content with what he had and always made the most of things. For instance, he loved eating, he loved to sit in his armchair every evening and fall asleep with the paper, and he especially loved those operas of his; he used to listen to them and sing along from morning to night and, well, we did think it was a bit much at times but we kept our mouths shut, why shouldn't he have a bit of pleasure? There are some husbands, after all, who squander half their pay on the lottery and suchlike, or who are crazy about football, and with him it was his operas. You must agree, sir, that it's a refined hobby. And also, he loved to make people laugh, he was a champion joker, he was the king of practical jokes, you may not believe this but just the morning of the day it happened, barely three hours before, he was making omelettes for the girls and he pretended to swallow the hot oil straight from the frying pan. What a fright we had before we started to laugh. What else can I say to you, sir, people are a riddle, even the ones you think you know best. You sleep in the same bed together for thirty-five years, you know every hair on their head, their illnesses, their secrets, their problems, their most personal things, and then suddenly it turns out that. It's as if there was two Elimelechs, one for foreign affairs and one for internal affairs. It was nice of you to come. Thank you. We'll do our best. The girls are just wonderful, look how they take after him. They take everything as it comes. When you next see Albert say a big thank you to him for taking the trouble to come to the funeral. He's not a youngster any more, and it's a long way from Bat Yam, after all.

Duet

Behind the first stream another rivulet is hiding.
The first one flows so loudly
that you can hardly hear the murmur
of the second, hidden one. Rico is sitting on a rock. Perhaps
you can only hear it in the dark? He is willing to wait.

The well-fed dog and the hungry dog

If you are Giggy Ben-Gal, a man who helps himself with both hands because
you only live once, for whom toys and pleasures and fun wink
from every branch as though it's Christmas all year round, earning your living
as a security adviser while maintaining dovish views, attending
the occasional rally and signing every petition, with a flat and car provided
by your parents who aren't short of a penny or two, and on the sweeter
side of life you have Ruthy Levin and Dita and another one, a married
woman, your friend's wife is your friend and anyway he has no idea (she's older
than you and full of surprises in bed), but at heart you're not selfish,
quite generous in fact, you enjoy fixing things for others, helping a friend
through a difficult patch, taking the weight off his shoulders, it's not
surprising that one fine evening you'll collar this Dombrov for a man-to-man
chat, to sort out what's really going on with this filmscript
that seems to have got stuck: after all, we're talking about relatively small
sums of money, and anyway you know a source you can tap.

And so you will sit facing one another in Café Limor, you cheery and brisk
while he looks bitter, careworn, not completely on the ball, for instance
when you say "grant" and he, instead of taking notes, starts describing Nirit.
Or if you imply that there's this fund you know of, he just stares abstractedly
into his beer then leans forward and downs it in one. For a moment you feel
disappointed, even hurt, is he really so ungrateful or has he just got
a screw loose? Suddenly you realize that the problem isn't the script, it's Dita.
The kid's jealous. He sits there wriggling on his chair, full of wretchedness
and shame, and at the same time he's drawn toward you, he doesn't dare
but he'd love to touch your hand that touches Dita and probably does things
to her, any way and any time it likes, that he can only dream of. He would

sell you a year of his fucked-up life here and now, just like that, for a hint
of a chance to taste just once a tiny crumb from your nightly feasts with her.
Sweeter even than her body for you now is his embittered envy, that
stimulates your complacency gland, and also makes you feel pity and an urge
to share your bread with the hungry, to grant him an evening with her,
a secret gift or a donation of surplus goods. There's also a surprising
pang of jealousy at the poor sod, with that desperate thirst of his
that someone like you has never known and never will. Right now
you're feeling thirsty too, so you order two more big frothy beers.

Stabat Mater

But why do you keep worrying? Calm down. See for yourself
how well I'm looking after myself,
I'm eating, sleeping, wrapping up warm in my sleeping-bag,
protecting myself from the freezing
breath of the winds, I even drink fresh mountain goats' milk
for breakfast. I won't get lost.

It's no good. She's all around me. She's worried. She's found
a hole in the elbow of my sweater, the soles of my boots
are worn too thin, and what's that cut on my cheek? She lays
a cold hand on my forehead
and another on her own, compares, naturally I'm warmer.
She doesn't trust me.

And why did you forget to send your father a postcard every week?
It's not so easy for him there,
looking after your girlfriend, well not exactly looking after her,
she's not exactly the one who's being looked after. In your place
I'd go back. You've checked out all these mountains one by one,
and it's nearly autumn,

it's time to go home. The mountains will always be here,
but your life won't. Instead of wandering around you could
be an architect for instance: what with your father's way with a balance sheet,
my gift for embroidery, your grandfather who was a silversmith, and Uncle
Michael, the pharmacist, put it all together and you'll be a master architect.
Take a rest, Mother, I say to her. Sit down for a bit. You're tired.

You've worried enough. Go back to sleep
curled up like a fetus in the hammock of the deep.
Master architect, doctor, they're
marketable professions. But every market closes in the end,
and everything perishes,

dust to dust. Suppose your son puts Number One first,
so the whole of Bat Yam is full of his glory and all the substance
of his house, a name and legacy, a Mercedes and precious unguents,
surely with the passing of the years all will be covered in dust.
The name will fade, the unguents will dry up and only a powdery crust
will remain and it too in the end will fly

to the four winds. A forgotten, invisible, imperceptible powder, Mother,
the dust of forsaken
collapsed buildings, shifting sands swept by the wind,
ashes returning to ashes,
from a handful of cosmic dust our planet was formed,
and to a black hole it shall return.

A doctor an architect in a dream house with fancy carpets
in the best part of Bat Yam. Powder.
Rest in your peace, Mother, after the mountains I shall come
and you and I shall hide
beyond reach of the cloud that existed before anything was made
and that when all has passed away shall be alone.

Comfort

Shortly before sunset Albert walks round to Bettine's to seek her advice
on a particular case involving double taxation. Bettine is pleased to see him
but hasn't got time to talk, she has her grandchildren with her, she is three,
he is one-and-a-bit, she is drawing a palace and he has crawled into
a cardboard box hideaway. Bettine offers some homemade lemonade
to Albert, who, carried away, is already down on all fours giving a recital
of animal and bird noises but the lion strikes the wrong note,
the tot in the box is scared, tears, and a bottle for comfort. Albert too seems
chastened and in need of comfort, so the little girl offers him a present,
the palace, on condition he don't cough scare no more. Later, in the empty
alley on his way back to Amirim Street a bird on a branch calls to him.
With no living soul to hear he replies and this time he hits the right note.

Subversion

Bettine likes to sit indoors in the evening
in her pleasant room that faces the sea, half-submerged in potted plants,
wearing a summer kimono, her still-shapely legs
propped up on a footstool.

She is deep in a novel about a divorce and an error.
The suffering of the fictional characters fills her
with a feeling of calm. As though their burden has fallen
from her own shoulders.

Yes, she too is getting older, but without feeling
humiliated by it. A senior civil servant of sixty,
with her bobbed hair and those earrings, she feels
younger than her age.

The sea that is close to her home seeps through her windows
and inside her body too there is a murmur
seductively, secretly pleading with her, like a little child
lightly pulling at her sleeve.

What is this body after? One more game?
Another outing? Let me rest. It's late.
But it pleads persistently,
not knowing when to give up.

She glances at her watch: what now? Go out? To Albert?
Who was here not two hours ago? It's late. It's absurd.
And that girl is still there, and there is, after all, something
cheap about her.

Exile and kingdom

Something cheap and something soft and something hard and remote,
Dita Inbar in her orange uniform, with a name-badge on the lapel,
works three nights a week as a receptionist at an expensive seaside hotel,
tourists, investors, philanderers, foreign airline pilots in uniform
and teams of tired stewardesses. Forms. Credit cards.
At four in the morning she has some free moments for a casual chat
with the Narrator, who is staying here after a lecture at the expense
of the sponsoring organization (it is not easy for him to drive all the way back
to Arad so late at night on his own). But he can't sleep. In a fit
of hotel depression he goes downstairs and paces the lobby, where
he finds you at the desk, looking official, tired but pretty.
Good evening. Evening? It's nearly morning. What's it like
here? Do you take in stray birds? What do you mean birds—
corpses more like. Have you ever seen a face reflected in a spoon? That's
what the whole human race looks like after midnight. Aren't you
the author? A friend of mine reads your books.
The only one I've read is *To Know A Woman*. But what a woman is
the hero hardly knows. Maybe you don't either. Men
are mostly wrong, whether they're authors or not. Tell you the truth,
I write too. Not books, screenplays, just for my own amusement so far.
Shall I send you one? Would you read it? You must be drowning
in manuscripts. How about yourself? Got another
book on the way? Don't suppose you'll tell me what it's about?
If it weren't for the years and my fame and a fear of being made a fool of
I'd stand here, a desk's width away from your body, and tell you
about Nirit, *narimi*, Bhutan, and the cross on the way. Nearly.
But not quite. While you smile at me all of a sudden

both phones call you at once. I too
fake a smile, return a vague wave of the hand, and walk away
to stand at the big window overlooking the sea. It has been written
that exile is a kingdom and it's been written that it is a fleeting
shadow. A filthy old dog is this September dawn, dusty, yawning
on the seashore, limping among the dustbins.

An ugly bloated baby

After his mother became ill Rico stayed out quite a lot. It was useless his father pleading with him. That winter he came home at two o'clock almost every night. Only rarely did he sit by the invalid's bedside. The selfish love of an only child. Sometimes when he was little he used to imagine that his father had gone away, that he had been sent to Brazil, or moved in with another woman, and the two of them were left on their own in a pleasantly enclosed life, consoling each other. At least he wanted all the traffic between his parents to flow through his own junction and not through a tunnel behind his back. Her illness seemed to him as though she had suddenly had a baby daughter, a demanding pampered creature, a little like him, it was true, but a spoilt child. He imagined that if he went away his mother would have to choose between the two of them, and he was sure she would never give him up. How astonished he was when she eventually chose the ugly bloated baby and left him alone with his father.

Soon

At the beginning of this autumn, like every year, I planted some
chrysanthemums next to the bench in the garden. And like every year
I had my hair cut at Chez Gilbert for Hanukkah and then I went shopping to
fill the gaps and replace some worn-out items on my shelf of flannel nighties,
and got home in time to light the first candle with Albert, because Dita
had rung to say sorry but she and Rico couldn't make it. It seems likely I
won't live to see the end of this winter. Dr. Pinto is optimistic, the situation
seems stable, if anything the left one is a little less good, but the right one
is clear and there are no secondaries. They even see some improvement there.
So the story moves on with intervals that are getting longer every time,
because I tire easily. Meanwhile I continue embroidering a place mat
that I'd like to finish. I rest every ten minutes, my fingers are turning white
and my eyes see things that aren't there. Sometimes I'm so terrified of it
like a pack of wolves and sometimes I just wonder how exactly it will come.
Is it like falling asleep? Like being burnt? Sometimes I regret we didn't take a
second trip last summer to Crete, where night fell so slowly and the salt smell
mingled with the tang of the pines and we drank wine with ewes' milk cheese
while the shadow of the mountains spread right across the plain but the
mountains themselves were still illuminated in the distance by a light that
promised that peace would come and the water in the stream was icy
even though it was August. Sometimes there's a pain and I lie down at once,
take a pill, I don't even wait the ten minutes I promised Dr. Pinto. He surely
won't be angry. And I sometimes feel something I can't remember the
word for, *tmno*, is it "dark"? My Hebrew is abandoning me, and making room
for more and more Bulgarian. Which is coming back to me now. Rico will
come back too, even though it's past two o'clock, and Albert is waiting on
the veranda, fuming, now he has come back inside and is holding my feet.

He is holding me firmly and warmly and it really is soothing even though I was calm already. Maybe this death is a Japanese? A sort of samurai. Mannered. Hiding behind a childish ritual mask, a smooth shiny mask. The unwrinkled cheeks are not even snowy-white but china-white, the cheeks look powdered and the brow seems polished. The mouth turns downward at the corners and there are long narrow empty cracks for eyes. It's really a baby. If so it is rather terrifying, precisely because this china-white mask is so smooth and expressionless. If it is a woman, it's strange that she hasn't noticed there's a fried fish in the frying pan in the kitchen, cold and hard from this morning. If it really is a baby, there's a diaper here; they put it between my head and the pillow to soak up the perspiration. And if behind the china mask there is a wrestler, a sumo wrestler, a Japanese weight-lifter, what he will find at his feet is a body wrapped in a sheet. Albert turned up the heater for me and now it's too hot, I'm soaking, and he's gone outside again, waiting on the veranda to tell Rico off the moment he gets back. Should I take a nap? Not yet. It's a pity to miss details and soon the bird.

Rico shouts

But dont you let it Mother bite and scratch
youre so submissive and obedient dont you let
so cold and evil crouching over you undoing and ripping
your pale skin your breasts
youre blind youre not in Crete youre not
among the streams and mountains dont you let
it Mother dont be gentle with it it will tear
your flesh and chew you to the bone
ripping and sucking the marrow of your spine so shout

so cold and evil crouching over you tearing and preying
forcibly planting in your womb a monster a bloated baby
shout out dont let it Mother bite kick and scratch
gouge its eyeballs out so obedient cotton wool
bite and scratch dont lie down so submissively dont let it
feast on your flesh relishing you all bit by bit
yes rip it gouge it yes tear its eyes out so shout

its crouching to dismember you liver pancreas and kidney
seeping into your spleen tearing you creeping from ovary
to gut sucking and chewing at your diaphragm
planting venomous fangs into lung and palate fight it
my chewed mother get it by the throat dont let it
Mother slain lamb shout.

A hand

It's a little less hot today which is why I asked him to come and sit with me on the veranda from where we can see the garden and breathe the nearby sea. This summer is already trailing signs of tiredness but it is still cruel and changeable, a capricious old tyrant. I put two liter bottles of mineral water on the table, remembering from last time how insatiably thirsty he is. The tax file he brought with him seems, at first glance, not entirely above board, it is sloppy and may have cut a few corners. Dombrov is a small company producing mainly advertisements and short public information films, the risk of fires in summer, the importance of wearing a seat belt. I'll go over it for him. Put it straight. It's a matter of two or three hours' work. And in the meantime the sea breeze comes and goes. On the garden seat below us a black cat lay dozing. Once again he talked about chance and guiding hands, like the first morning. It was not chance, in his view, that brought Dita and him together. Would it seem absurd if he confided in me that her script exactly describes his life and even his most intimate fantasy? A quiet house in a village, adjacent to a cemetery, with a tiled roof and thirty or forty fruit trees, a dovecote and a beehive, all surrounded with a stone wall and shaded by tall cypresses, and a young woman, Nirit, who because of a moment of compassion or some other fleeting emotion comes to stay for a few days, despite the fact that women usually find him repulsive. That is her script in a nutshell and it exactly represents the fantasy that has haunted him for many years, and that he has never told to another man or woman. It's a fact. Is it really possible, Mr. Danon, that it's just coincidence? How on earth did she manage to write a stranger's innermost dream? And another mysterious thing, how do you explain that she brought this script to me of all people? Half the inhabitants of Tel Aviv are producers. Or think they are. Do you really believe, Mr. Danon, that it's all just coincidence?

To this, naturally, I neither had nor could have an answer one way or the other—who can say—however I was surprised that this time, unlike his previous visit, he did not touch the glass of water I had poured him, which fountained bubbles excitedly till it grew tired, and subsided. As though in the meantime he had undergone a thorough detox. Instead, while he was expounding his views on probability, he attacked the fruit I had put in front of him, pears, grapes, apples, and devoured it without noticing what he was doing, munching, dripping, unaware that he was staining his clothes, what is just chance, Mr. Danon, and what is the result of the guiding hand of fate? I was astonished that he attributed some kind of decisive authority to me of all people. If we had lived let's say a couple of hundred years ago you might have imagined that he had come to me to ask for her hand in marriage and meanwhile here he was beating about the bush.

It's not easy to know, I said, whether there is such a thing as a guiding hand, and it's even harder to explain towards what and to what purpose this hand, if it exists, is or is not guiding what appears to us as chance. I sometimes wonder myself. To be sure what I said did not contain any answer, but somehow he seemed satisfied, even happy: on hearing the words "I sometimes wonder myself" his greedy mole's face suddenly lit up, and for an instant through this expression I caught a glimpse of a sad, unloved child, whose father has suddenly given him an unexplained pat on the back, that he has interpreted as a caress. Before I had any notion where or why, my hand reached out, touched him lightly on the shoulder as I saw him to the door, and "Don't worry," I said, but why did I say it, "we'll check through your tax papers and maybe straighten them out a bit, get in touch next week and don't even mention money."

Chandartal

It drips. It stops. It trickles.
The water tastes like wine.
A sluggish little fountain
in the courtyard of the shrine.

We've reached Ladakh, the "country
of the children of the moon,"
along the River Chandar,
and a lake named Chandartal.

The village is called Tiksa,
Tiksa Gumpa is the shrine,
the woman's name, Maria: you're
the one that she recalls.

The one who kissed her feet.
Yes, I mean you: come here.
Did you know there is a custom
in the region of Ladakh

to give one bride in marriage
to two or three young men,
to two or three young brothers.
It's you that she recalls.

The fountain flows and falters,
it stops and starts again
in the courtyard of the shrine.

The stone here is not chiselled,
but plastered white and red.
The shrine is Tiksa Gumpa,
the woman Maria. Come

to me. Fear not. I'm talking
to you. Tonight my lips
you shall open. Tonight
I'll be with you. Tiksa Gumpa
is the shrine and the lake is
Chandartal.

What never was and has gone

Maria too is lost, she roams from shrine to shrine,
sleeps, rises, packs her bag, sometimes in the company
of wayfaring men. Her beauty is wearing thin. Her face
is wrinkled by wind, sun and frost. The promised land
has gone or was it just a mirage? Whatever she has given
has been taken, and whatever is left will perish.

Promised lands are a lie. There is
no wondrous snowman in the mountain ravines. Only
in the sea there awaits her what never was
and has gone. Tonight the boy is with her.
Tomorrow alone. Chandartal.

Get out

Voices he hears, Tatars. What Tatars. Which Tatars.
Tatars in his head. Come back tomorrow, preferably
in a different frame of mind. Come back without the voices.
Without the Tatars. Without the torture. He is dead,
Elimelech the carpenter. On the windowsill a candle burns,
for the end of Sabbath or for remembrance. Who is crying
shouting Tatars to distinguish between weekday and
disaster? Elimelech the carpenter is dead hanged in the shed in the yard
looking like a practical joke, it was Rajeb who found him. Nine years on
and tomorrow his daughter is to be wed, I am invited to the wedding
and preferably in a different frame of mind. She is marrying
a land dealer around Nablus and they are settling
in Elon Moreh. Where are these omens coming from?
Tatars. Candle in the window. Elimelech the carpenter taught Rajeb
to sing duets with him, basso profundo and tenor, both
out of tune. Four armed settlers will support the posts
of her bridal canopy and you will stand with Albert
who is coming from Bat Yam. Palely the carpenter's daughter
smiles. The bridal veil is very fine. A bunch of roses
and a well-fed bridegroom. Sabbath end? Remembrance? And the rabbi
leaps and dances Tatars. Get out. What Tatars. Where
are the omens coming from and who is calling me where?
The carpenter hanged himself and Rajeb returned to Hebron.
He has not been seen since. Some say he ran away to Sudan
others that he was caught or killed constructing an explosive device,
and others are Tatars. Thick darkness and a candle outside the hired hall.
A car park. Silence. Dogs barking in the distance at a moon
that does not answer. Get out. Cut your roots and go.

Only the lonely

Evening and she has not come. Next door a child is crying, tiredly,
monotonously, knowing that nothing will help. In the one-room flat
I have rented for her in Mazeh Street there is no phone yet. And even
if there were I wouldn't. This evening she won't come. On my own eating
black bread, cheese and olives. It's a long evening. Everyone is on his own
this evening and I too am on my own. I am wondering whether the money I
sent has reached you. Anxious about avalanches, landslides on those slopes.
Or awake, reading by candlelight in the cold in an abandoned temple. The
evening is still. The child who was crying before is quiet now. Here at my
kitchen window the sea is talking about autumn already. Another glass of tea
and I'll sit down to check a balance sheet that doesn't balance. Many send in
their accounts. Only the lonely know how to be accurate.

Rico feels

Yes the night is really cold and the snow reminds him of his father.
It creeps like a tiny furry creature
slinking across the valley.

Quiet and even, it gropes at the roof and the walls.
In the dark the sleepwrapped snow on tiptoe,
silent and anxious, spreads a blanket over him.

And the same evening Dita too

In a foam-filled bath
she pities their loneliness:
one wanted me to mother him
the other looks to me as a daughter.
To be a woman to both of them
is something I can only do in the bath.

A wish stirs

Evening. Rain falls on the empty desert hills. Chalk and flint and the smell
of dust being wetted after an arid summer. A wish stirs: to be
what I would have been had I not known what is known. To be before
knowledge. Like the hills. Like a rock on the surface of the moon.
Simply there, motionless, and trusting
in the length of its shelf life.

I think

Night. In the garden ploughs a breeze. A cat,
I think a cat, pads among bushes, a shadow
flitting among the shadows. It sniffs or guesses
something hidden from me. What is not mine to sense
is taking shape there now without me. Cypresses
tremble slightly, black, in a motion of mourning,
I think beside the wall. Something there is touching
some other thing. Something is expiring. Ostensibly
all this is taking shape right before my eyes
as I watch the garden from this window. So I think.
In fact all this has always happened and always will
but only ever behind my back.

A web

Waking tired at twenty to five. Lights. A pee. A wash. Then standing
with a coffee at the window. Chilly mist still in the bushes. The garden
light continues signalling to itself. The lawn is still damp.
Empty. Chairs, with legs in the air, upside down on the garden table.
There is a milky light
toward dawn, lest we forget that we are in
the Milky Way, a remote galaxy flickering until it fades out.

Until it fades out five-o'clock-in-the-morning things are happening. A
startled bird calls out in surprise, as though this were the very first morning.
Or the very last. Between two branches of a ficus an early spider is at work.
From the humors of its body it spins a tight net in which it hunts
twenty or thirty dewdrops that do not sit idle either but catch splinters
of light and multiply each one sevenfold. Every captive splinter, for its part,
translates itself to lightning. Until the paper arrives I'll sit down and write too.

Rico thinks about the mysterious snowman

Man that is born of woman bears his parents on his shoulders. No, not on
his shoulders. Within him. All his life he is bound to bear them,
together with all their host, their parents, their parents' parents,
a Russian doll heavy with child back to the first generation:
wherever he walks he bears his forebears, when he lies down he bears
his forebears and when he rises up he bears them, or if he wanders far or
stays in his place. Night after night he shares his cot with his father
and his couch with his mother until his day comes.

But that snowman is not born of woman. Weightless and naked
it roams alone on the barren mountains. Neither born nor begetting
neither loving nor thirsty for love. It has never mourned
nor lost a living soul. Ageless it floats over the snows,
fatherless, motherless, homeless, timeless and deathless. Alone.

One by one

He rolls down the woman Maria's stockings, one by one, his eyes
digging into her flesh. These are the eyes of the flesh. The eyes
of his spirit are closed. Were they not closed he would see Maria not
in her ripe sensuality but as she will look in old age, shrivelled like a
dried fig. If he opened the eyes of his spirit the desires of the flesh
would subside. His lust would turn to dust.

Or it could be put like this: climbing a tortuous track in the mountains,
between two chasms. His glance is alert and sharp but the eyes of his spirit
are shut. If he opens them just for an instant, he will feel dizzy and fall.

All this is ancient knowledge: the eyes of the flesh covet, the eye of the spirit
goes dark, he who is here is you without you, he who is not
here is not here, but if so why love a woman? Why walk across chasms?

Your son longs

Your son longs for the extinction of sleep. And at once
he sleeps. The wind outside the hut
howls. A fox slinks by in the wood
and there is a night bird hidden in the leaves
seeing what is coming but choosing to pass over

in silence. In seventeen hundred and six
a wandering merchant from Russia who was on his way to China
breathed his last in this hut. He died
alone in his sleep and was buried in the wood
where he sank into the depth of oblivion.

A wandering merchant from Russia who was on his way to China

to take furs and precious stones from Nizhni to Nanking, and from Nanking
brought back jewelery and silk. He was fond of drinking and eating at
wayside inns, strange travellers' tales at night in front of a blazing fire,
and servant girls' favors on a straw palliasse by the light of a clay lamp.
He took pleasure in shrewd selling and in haggling for a bargain, fine
patient dealing, resembling courtship, or loveplay in which
he who lasts longest wins, and the swift have no advantage: he who desires
must feign indifference and cloak his eagerness with uncertainty. In the spring
he set his steps eastward and returned homeward in the fall, crossing
rivers and forests, steppes and mountain passes, and every year
the hoard of coins buried in his courtyard grew and grew.

One evening, in this hut, he ate his fill till midnight, paid
a girl to wait on his couch and warm his bedding,
and, when she had left, he settled comfortably on his back
to count and calculate how much he had gained this year,
how much the next would bring, and how much more
he would accumulate in the course of the decade. Until his eyelids
dropped and he slept and at daybreak the servant girl
shook his shoulders to no avail, so she raised her voice and cried,
frightening all the village. All this happened long ago
and has long since been forgotten. Soon you too.

It's not a matter of jealousy

Good evening, this is Bettine speaking, I'm a friend of Albert Danon. We met a couple of times while you were staying with him but we didn't talk much: we didn't get the chance, or perhaps we felt awkward. I hesitated for a long time before calling you. I hope I'm not disturbing you. And you're perfectly entitled to say, Look, it's none of your business. Or even to hang up. I'll understand. The thing is this: you moved into his flat as his son's girlfriend, or ex-girlfriend, I'm not asking and you don't have to answer. Either way, he took you in and got you out of trouble and apparently he even ended up finding you or helping you to find a place of your own. I don't know the details and I don't want to. He is a generous and efficient man in his quiet way. But you, whether deliberately or not, are doing something bad to him. I use the present tense because even now that you've moved to wherever you've moved to, he's still unsettled because of you or else not because of you but, let's say, in your wake. Wait. Don't interrupt me. This conversation is not exactly easy for me as it is. I'm very concerned that you don't misunderstand me. I don't want to be judgmental and I'm certainly not trying to tell you off but merely to advise you, not even advise you really but simply to ask you to give it some thought. You're a good-looking young woman and you belong to a generation where certain things have become quite simple, perhaps too simple. I'm not passing judgment, I'm merely voicing an impression that may be groundless. I'm older than you, possibly older than your mother, so it's not a matter of jealousy or competition. Surely you too— but no, I don't want to get into that, and please consider what I have just said unsaid, because even a denial of jealousy is liable to arouse suspicion. Let me try putting it this way: He is grieving for his wife, and on top of that, as you know, he is upset that his son has gone away. Even though he's by no means a weak man, you will surely agree with me that it is not necessary to add to his pain. When you were staying in his flat he was almost looking for somewhere to run away to, whereas now that you've left it's all he can do to stop himself from going to look for you, because you promised to visit him and you forgot. No, don't apologize, you're busy, of course I understand, a girl your age and so on. I'm sorry. Just give me another minute or two and I'll stop. What I wanted to say, or rather ask, is that you shouldn't leave him hanging in mid-air. He doesn't sleep at night and he looks as though he may be getting ill. You have caused a misunderstanding, and you are the only person who can clear it up. Apart from which, you may not have thought about what will happen when Rico comes back. What sort of relationship will you have with the two of them, and what sort of relationship will they have with each other? Forgive me for raising these questions, I have been a civil servant for thirty-eight years, and I may have picked up a rather bureaucratic tone. I'm not asking you to break off relations or disappear but rather—how should I put it—to observe some boundaries. Perhaps I have not succeeded in explaining myself. I feel the need to say to you, Look, Dita, you arouse something in him that makes him very sad, depressed, you may not even have noticed, but if you want to put it right you'll have to draw some lines. No. That wasn't quite what I wanted to say to you, and it may have sounded petty. It's hard for me to find the words. One weekend, many years ago, my husband Avram and I took Albert and Nadia for a day trip to Upper Galilee. At dusk we saw, all four of us, a furry creature scurry down a slope and vanish among some trees. We tried to keep it in sight but it had vanished. The sun went down and for a long time afterwards it seemed as though the whole world was shimmering and would go on shimmering for ever. Albert said it was definitely a stray dog, and Nadia said it was a wolf. It was a pointless argument, because look what has happened since: Avram died long ago, and now Nadia has died, and the wolf or dog is dead too. Only Albert and I are still alive. By my reckoning you may not even have been born the evening that I've remembered all these years, with no pain now but with a clarity that gets sharper and sharper with the passage of time. A wolf or a stray dog? The wood was in darkness and there were Albert and I confronting Avram and Nadia in an argument that had no ending and could not have any, the creature had vanished into the dark and around us everything was empty and silent and shimmering. You must understand, I've told you this story not to make you feel uncomfortable but only to make a request, or rather to convey to you what I am asking myself and that is why I am asking you too. You don't have to answer. Naturally, all this will remain just between you and me. Or rather, between you and yourself.

It's only because of me that it came back to her

She says she's not jealous. Like hell she's not. Not angry.
Like hell she's not. She's right as rain but in fact
when all's said and done, she only wants him for herself. She wants me
to get out of his sight this minute, draw a line as she puts it,
or else she'll gouge my eyes out. It's my fault
he doesn't sleep. So what if he doesn't sleep. Being awake is being alive.
If I weren't around, by now he'd probably be dozing
for hours on end in an armchair or sitting on his veranda staring ahead
for a month, a winter, a year, gradually the sea would come up
to his head. Hers too. Instead of bugging me
she should actually say thank you nicely:
it's only because of me that it came back to her, that stray dog in Galilee
or that shimmering wolf, or whatever it was.
It's only because of me that what was almost blacked out is shimmering again
for her as well as for him. I'm quite fond of him. But not of her.
Not at all.

Every morning he goes to meet

As for the Narrator, on these late September days he gets up each morning
before five and writes for an hour or so until the paper arrives. Then
he goes outside to check if there is anything new in the desert. To date
there is nothing. The mountains to the east are stamped out
against the sky. Every slope in its proper place. Like yesterday. And
the day before. That lizard, a pocket dinosaur, has not improved
his position. The Narrator is interested in registering all this, in trying
to clarify and record here what has been and what is. Things must be
called by their proper names or by another name that sheds a fresh light
or casts, here and there, some shadow. Fifty years have passed:
in Jerusalem, on Zechariah Street, in a two-room flat, a private
school belonging to Mrs. Yonina. My teacher was Mrs. Zelda, Zelda
who some years later wrote the poems in *The Spectacular Difference* and *The
Invisible Carmel.* Once, on a winter day, she chose to say
to me softly: If you stop talking sometimes
maybe things will sometimes be able to talk to you. Years later
I found it promised in one of her poems that *trees and stones
will respond Amen.* A spectacular difference she promised,
between stones and trees, to anyone who is prepared to listen.

What I wanted and what I knew

I can still remember her room.
Zephaniah Street. A back entrance.
A frenetic boy, seven and a quarter.
A word-child. A suitor.

My room does not ask, she wrote,
for sunrise or sunset. Enough
that the sun brings its tray of gold
and the moon its tray of silver. I remember.

Grapes and an apple she gave me
in the summer holidays of '46.
I sprawled on the rush matting,
a fib-child. And in love.

From paper I used to cut her
flowers and blossoms. A skirt
she had, a brown one, like herself,
a bell and a smell of jasmine.

A soft-spoken woman. I touched
the hem of her dress. By chance.
What I wanted I didn't know
and what I knew still hurts.

De profundis

What I knew still hurts. Nadia Danon, for instance: like my teacher Zelda
she too died of cancer. Despite the bird before dawn, despite embroidering
until two days before she died, despite Dr. Pinto mercifully drugging her,
a false hope deluded her. Struck roots inside her. Refused to let go.

The twilight of her suffering showed her a samurai in a china mask, who was
her first husband: a tall, stern, elegant man, who always knew what was right,
he would turn out the light, curl up, press her breast, burrow and fiddle
in her flesh, hurting her to the bone but in the end he always let go. Soon
he had had enough of her and she was saved. Not long now.

Giggy responds

But what if anything would Giggy Ben-Gal say about all this? This story
is getting on his nerves, because the night is still young and there are
some juicy scenes still to come, women going down, shares going up
tonight he has plenty of tricks to turn. Tel Aviv is a big pond,
where he plays step by step, one move at a time.
Joking aside though, the bastard who laughs last laughs longest. In
less than a year he'll be number two in the firm,
and then he'll really hit the town, *the sky is the limit*
*and the limit is just the first step.** Those bad scenes, like sickness
suffering and death, are strictly for the losers who are stuck on
the south side of town. Lonely people
deserve to live alone, and the needy deserve to be poor. Life
may or may not be a picnic but, on the other hand, even your Mr. Perfect
is really just another show-off. Everyone pisses and fucks so why should they
all pretend otherwise, that frustrated Narrator and the other old moralizers.

*English in the original.

Dies irae

A short time before or after sunset this Narrator goes outside to check
what is going on and if there is any news in the desert. The wind
is always leaving: it always blows from there to there,
through here but never from here. A dust devil rises, dissolves and
re-forms on another hill. And disappears again. One move
at a time, he laughs last, the gospel according to Giggy Ben-Gal. Suffering
sickness and death come and go. Unlike this desert. Unlike the stars
in the sky. They are fixed. But this too is only apparent. Better a living dog,
and the poor man's wisdom is poor, a barren heath in the desert which the
wind stirs up then abandons. Always abandons. It comes from there and
drifts to there, it whirls around and returns into stillness. It is not the dead
who will see it, and sweet is the light to the eyes.

My hand on the latch of the window

Dear parents, dear Fania and Arie, it's night now and I'm in my room
in Arad, alone with my tea and these pages. The requiem is by Fauré. A fan
is whirring, blowing, turning away, coming back. The desert
is empty and near. At the windows the darkness is warm. And you
are both resting in peace. Are you sleeping? Or quarrelling still? At least
you can't fight over me: I'm tidy, hard-working, successful. Bringing you
more and more pride and joy, a regular sorcerer's apprentice. I'm tired
but I never give up. You both wanted me to grow up to be one thing
or another. Dad one thing and Mother another.
Now the difference is gradually shrinking. What difference does it make
what I am. I shall be here for a little while longer, and then I shall rest.
It's late. This street is empty and the garden is whispering to itself
in Russian, so I won't understand. It's mistaken: at this hour secrets
are less secret and almost all things are revealed. For years and years
Dad you stockpiled footnotes while you, Mother, stood at the window,
clutching your usual lemon tea, with your back to the room. Tormenting
yourself and longing like Elimelech the carpenter to return to some orchard
you'd dreamed up. Which never existed. Whispering to each other
in Russian which sounds soft and deadly. Dad you stand up,
stooped. Mother you are sitting, erect and beautiful. Dad you appear to
insist, refusing to open the window. But you Mother won't give in.
In the deep darkness you weep in vain in a whisper,
in whispers Dad you try to explain. My hand on the latch of the window, I
must now choose. If I am to forgive, then this is the moment.

And you

Piercing, despairing, in Yiddish, the sound in the distance of a woman
whose child in front of her eyes and she screams.
Then a wailing in Arabic, of a woman
whose home. Or whose child. Her voice is penetrating, terrifying. And you
sharpen a pencil or repair a torn dust jacket. At least
you could shudder.

The hart

As the hart pants after the water brooks, so does my soul. And a pair
of dark cypresses sway to and fro in wordless devotion. As the waters
cover the sea, the proud waters have gone over it: they passed over
and are gone and are no more. Return unto your rest my soul. Where
is your rest? Where will you return to, for what will you pant like a hart?
The kettle whistles. Time for coffee. If the light that is in you be darkness,
how great is that darkness. A fly is trapped between
the window pane and the screen. The house is empty.
A rug. A curled cat. When shall I come, when shall I appear?
The light is darkness. There was a hart at the water and it has gone.

At the end of the jetty

And on the first rainy day, with a grey peaked cap, a raincoat and an umbrella, and a brown bundle firmly secured with string, Albert Danon caught two buses to go from Amirim Street to Mazeh Street to see how his son's girlfriend was doing. Under his sleeve, under his watch strap, he carefully tucked the two punched tickets. He looked like a retired schoolmaster. Waiting for the red light to change to green even though the street was empty. Crossing Rothschild Boulevard, picking up a sodden newspaper from a bench and dropping it into a litter bin. Tel Aviv in the first rain looks like a heap of jetsam. The streets are deserted: anyone who has anywhere to go has gone. In Mazeh Street there's an impression of fallen leaves: fallen plaster, fallen papers mixed with some brown leaves and soggy rubbish. Everything is soaked but not washed clean. On the rooftops antennae, solar water heaters and clouds. The birds are there but their singing is flattened. And in the unlit entrance is a row of mailboxes, Cherniak, Shikorsky, Benbassat and a private neurological clinic. On the left-hand door on the ground floor, a note: "The podiatrist is out of the country." On the door opposite was written Inbar. No Dita: just Inbar. Like a man. A stranger. Forsaken like a winter sea, this stairwell. Albert Danon, a thin, elderly man, stands staring at the end of the jetty as though waiting for the black water to give up a life raft. He presses a bell. Which does not work. A polite interval. He presses again. Hesitates. Taps softly on the door. Waits again. Maybe she is getting dressed? Or she's asleep? Or she's not alone? He puts his bundle down on the floor and rests his umbrella. He waits. And in the meantime he wipes his feet in front of her door so as not to bring any water or dead leaves inside. He waits. Inside the bundle there is a flannel nightdress of Nadia's and an old two-bar electric heater. Albert blows into his hands, sniffs his breath, suddenly fearing it may smell bad. Then he knocks on the door again. And waits.

Passing through

Sit down Albert. Take off your coat.
Let's draw the curtain. Light the light.
I was asleep. What, never mind,

don't worry. It was time I woke.
I'll put some water on for coffee
and throw a bedspread over the mess.

I'll make us both some cheese on toast.
Thanks for the heater. And the nightie.
Your wife's. And what a pretty blue.

It may suit me some years from now.
Just wait there while I have a shower.
Or come with me. Take off your shoes.

And take that off, while I undress.
Now come with me. No, don't be shy.
There is a custom in Ladakh,

perhaps an ancient marriage law:
they marry three or four brothers
together to a single bride.

Three brothers. And a single bride.
Stop shivering, and touch me here.
Touch, it's not me, it's only cloth.

It's only cotton: touch me here.
Think that it's happening in a dream
high in the hills of Chandartal.

My fingers are like alleyways,
my palm's a square. You cross it, then
you stop. My arm is like a curving road,

my shoulder is a river bed and then
the neck's a bridge. Then you can choose
to go this way, or that. To wait. To wait.

In a dream in a cloud in passion
and wonder. Just listen to the thunder.

Then he walks around for a while and returns to Rothschild Boulevard

When he left, the rain had stopped. The boulevard was a girl
stripped naked and beaten up by a gang, and left lying there on her back
ripped and drenched. Now she hears trees,
promising her a kind of second silence, which belongs
at the end of shame and degradation, a still, small silence,
a kind of birth: I shall no longer raise my eyes to the hills
but lie quietly now in a puddle
of muddy still waters. Here is the breeze. Here are rumors
of birds' wings, stitching the damp air, unstitching,
restitching, unstitching again. Everything now is grey
and tender. Rest. In peace. Smelling sweetly
of good rain and earth. Everything is past.

Squirrel

Eyes. Eyes. Eyes in the water eyes in the branches eyes in the curtains eyes in the jug and eyes in the pillow. Nadia remembers Nadia as a little girl in an organdie frock or a pleated skirt, with ribbons in her plaits, Sabbath eve silver candlesticks warm hallah raisin wine blessings and table songs sit up straight please and stop squinting. She remembers gleaming white lace-trimmed napkins, porcelain bowls the color of the sea, a woven wall rug, little baskets, sauce boats, the smell of basil, lavender and ginger, and candied fruit. Eyes, eyes, and Nadia remembers squirrels in the branches of the deserted garden milky-white mist in the hills snow blossoming on a darkening meadow the poignant tolling of a bell at dusk, dark woods that whispered rumors when the wind blew, the howl of a wolf on a winter's night beyond the garden fence, the dovecote and the cockerel and the billy goat that frightened her in the dusk when she was sent out to fetch wood from the shed in the yard. Eyes in the water eyes in the night eyes eyes in my back, in my breasts, Nadia remembers old secrets, aged ten and a half in the morning, her father stripped to the waist up a ladder retiling the roof, and herself handing him up tiles one by one, inhaling the scent of his sweat and the sight of his nipples concealed in the steelwork of his chest bringing a secret trickle to her own ungrown nipples, she remembers the sudden flutter in her tummy and how the sun shone on his bare stooping back, as her father laid tile after tile and his muscles eyes eyes seemed to burrow between his shoulderblades. And once she watched her brother Michael hiding crouched in the back of the woodshed milking the dog's erection a blood-red butcher's-shop udder protruding horribly from the covering fur and the two of them, Michael and the dog, thirstily panting and lolling and then soft thunder rolled in her tummy and turning she ran from the woodshed and that same night the first blood appeared on her nightdress with her terrified tears and the pain as though a maggot had wriggled inside her. In a whisper her mother taught her how to and how not to and when, and how women hide their impurity from menfolk's eyes and how to smother the smell, and she also said that this was the curse of Eve: every woman is punished and sullied with blood, recompense for the serpent and apple, in sorrow shalt thou bring forth thy children and there is no way back and only in pregnancy and in old age do we get some relief. Eyes in the back eyes on the roof eyes on disgrace eyes on the festivals, Nadia remembers her handkerchiefs lace-edged brassières satin ribbons suspender belts translucent silk embroidered blouses corsets and headscarves, schemes and intrigues of virtuous women a cesspit concealed under layers of velvet, muffled laughter and sneers of old women leering aunts winking caressing deriding and gradually covering her with a silky cobweb of the spidery order of women, catching and trussing her in a network of transparent threads, initiating her by degrees into the mysteries of the sect, labyrinthine lies filigrees of guile a subversive sisterhood in the face of the male sex intrigues of ancient stratagems delicate perfumes, jewellery, cosmetics, eyes, eyes, evil eye. Nadia remembers a baby imprisoned in the underground lair of the priestesses of an all-female cult, rules of modesty, rules of menstrual impurity, rules of prudence, qualities of innocent cunning, powders and creams, eyeblack and rouge, the masculine nature you have to learn to arouse and to repel, grace is false and beauty is vain, but without them beware that you do not end up unwanted and dusty on the shelf, heaven forbid. Give them an inch and they take a mile, give them two inches and they'll cast you aside like an empty vessel, a woman is a pot filled to the brim with honey and shame, a locked garden and a reserved spring, a delight concealed until her redeemer cometh, no male stranger may approach, but neither should he be kept far off, keep him hungry and thirsty but occasionally feed him a crumb, cautiously always as if unawares lest you become a byword and a disgrace. Eyes, eyes, evil eye, amulets, giggles, whispers, intrigues, feminine plots and laws of womanhood, how to arouse love while preserving your modesty, dizzying incense, enchanting repulsion, she wanted to flee and she wanted to die, she wanted to run to the world of the squirrels to be for all time neither woman nor man but a tiny timorous creature which is all eyes and almost no body.

Never mind

But there, on the road to Patna, in the night train coming down from
the mountains, winding at a snail's pace into the valley, a shabby old train,
ancient carriages, wooden benches, and the engine fed on
sliced tree trunks, sparks flying by the window, swallowed up in
the depth of the darkness, faint lights in the distance, wretched villages,
mud huts, he thinks of writing a postcard to his father, and another
to Dita Inbar, to say to them both never mind. Tomorrow in Patna station
he will buy cards and stamps and post them. Never mind,
he wanted to say. Never mind that you took my father, such a thin,
childlike man, into the shower to see your body. Let him see it. Never
mind. I like the idea. And you took his hand and placed it here and there
to feel. Never mind that he saw you, never mind that he touched. After all,
he recoiled at once and fled to wander dazed on the boulevard among tattered
papers in the rain. No harm done. Never mind. After all, when I was a baby
his wife suckled me and changed my diaper, and lulled me to sleep on her
tummy, and now my wife does the same to him. Soon he will become a baby.

He adds sugar and stirs then adds more sugar

Dubi Dombrov is waiting at ten in the morning in Café Limor for a date which will never materialize because it has not been arranged. He leafs through a newspaper, glancing repeatedly at his watch as though she is already late. In fact his morning is fairly clear: there is nothing in his schedule except some postponed chores, insurance premiums, bills, a dermatologist's fee and accumulated parking tickets. On this December morning you can see, through the window, a pair of Russian girls by a road sign, laughing, ogling a biker in gloves and black leathers whose Suzuki roars between his thighs like a bull. At the entrance to the Odeon salon for "Bridal Styling—let us give you the finishing touch" stands a man in a dinner jacket and bow tie, wailing on a fiddle, his eyes seemingly closed. A penguin washed up in the Levant. There is also a grasshopper of a Hasid in the street, pestering passersby, soliciting them to put on *tefillin.* Dubi Dombrov, with a pale-green silk scarf round his neck, orders a cup of coffee with a slice of jam cake and fishes out the script of *Nirit's Love,* to polish it up: Far from the city far from Café Limor stands an old village house, adjoining the cemetery, with a tiled roof and chimney stack, thirty to forty fruit trees, some beehives and a dovecote, all surrounded with a stone wall, drowned in the shade of dense cypress trees. Here is where she will come for a few days and nights to sweeten his solitude. True, he is a pretty repulsive guy, that is why she feels sorry for him, but inside he is deep. Before her eyes, in the course of three days and nights, he will shine through brilliant and pure, he will slough off his hideous crust, be purged of the dross of defects, humiliations and lies, and stand before her like a candle whose light quivers gently among heaps of junk. Here in Café Limor, because of the low clouds, the shadow is gradually lapping up the puddles of feeble electric light as though sucking it up through a straw. Wait for me. Wait just a bit. Maybe this Giggy will wangle us a grant from that fund that his father is one of the trustees of, and you and I together will come up with a production that will leave everyone stunned and we'll walk away with a load of prizes and make tons of dough, and then you and I. Or else. Or I could drop everything and go off tomorrow to the Himalayas too, to shed my dead skin and set out in search of a spark. He pours another spoonful of sugar into his coffee, which has soaked up three spoonfuls already, stirs, and forgets to drink it. Should he go to her right now. Should he suggest that they make a fresh start. Wait for me. Wait just a bit. Or perhaps first he should send her a subtly worded love letter so she'll see he's not just another stud but above all a spiritual being. With thumb and forefinger he signals to the waiter to bring him a short espresso, and he continues to leaf through the script, sniffing and rooting around, leaving coffee stains on the pages and his sleeve, and pencilling notes in the margins, while his other hand absentmindedly adds sugar and stirs, then adds more sugar and stirs again.

Adagio

From morning to evening the light shines outside, not realizing
that it is light. Tall trees inhale silence with no need
to discover the essential essence of treedom. Empty steppes
stretch out forever on their backs without reflecting on
the pathos of their emptiness. Shifting sands shift and do not ask
how long or why or where to. All this wonderful existence is wonderful
but never wonders. The moon rises red, looking like a spilt eye,
searing the darkness of the sky, unsurprised by its own desolation. A cat
dozes on a wall. Dozing and breathing. Nothing more. Night after night
the wind whirls and blows over forests and hills. It whirls
continually. And blows. Not thinking and not appealing.
Only you, dust and humors, all night long you write
and erase, looking for a reason, a way to correct.

Nocturne

After the screw Giggy got up, put on a pair of sweat pants and
a shirt with a crocodile on it, picked up the phone,
and ordered a couple of speedy pizzas for Melchett 20, chop-chop.
She was wearing her jeans and his pullover. They laid the coffee table,
fork opposite knife, knife opposite fork, a pair of cups and two wine glasses.

The delivery boy sniffed the sweat of sex, stared at her with cuddly
puppy's eyes (she had forgotten to zip up her jeans). She felt sorry
for him, such a soulful, shy boy, she guessed at a mist of down
on his cheek that it would be quite nice to touch. Like a day-old chick. She
stood up. Took the boxes from him. She felt like letting him have. Just a kiss.

She stopped herself. At the door she touched his arm with her breast,
transmitted a spark and picked up a flicker, felt the scorch of an embarrassed
flame. When he had gone she sat down at the table. She saw a hair on her
plate. Hers? Giggy's? Or the boy's? The pizza was barely warm. The glass
had a gold band. Dita drank a little. Giggy winked at her, she nodded, not

necessarily at him. She pushed away her glass. Closed her eyes: there is a sea,
there are mountains. This flat is too chop-chop. The knife in his hand. The
fork in hers. Far from here there are forests. Rivers. Chandartal.
And darkness and winter and all their host too. You
are munching here and they stand silent. This fork is none too clean.

Meanwhile, in Bengal, the woman Maria

In a cheap room in a shabby inn she opens the window, leans out,
and fills her lungs with a cocktail of smells: mango blossom,
sewage, cooking odors, rotting fruit, cattle dung.

The night is tepid. The river is steaming. The darkness is bathed in faint decay.
In the cleft between her breasts Maria drips five or six drops of pungent
scent. She closes the window. Eats some fish. This fork is none too clean.

And seeing a fig tree afar off having leaves, he came, if haply he might find
any fruit on it: and when he came to it, he found nothing but leaves, for the time
of figs was not yet. She glances in the mirror. Eye pencil. Powder. Tissue.

Lipstick. If your right eye offends you. If salt loses its flavor. Changes
her skirt. Her client will be late. He will pay. Strip.
Demand in English to do it spoon-fashion,

like two spoons in a drawer. In this position
Maria feels swaddled, protected, not like
a harlot being taken but, so it seems for a moment,

as though her back is attached to the cross and the cross is united
with her flesh. And after that Jesus said to her, Go in peace my daughter
for thy demon hath departed. Then she showers, eats some toast,

and falls asleep with the threadbare acrylic doll from Italy
that has travelled with her from bed to bed. She dreams of bread
baked in a cottage. *Talitha numi*: sleep girl. Tomorrow, Chandartal.

Talitha kumi

Talitha kumi—get up girl, it's already half past nine. She works at the Hilton she's living in Mazeh she gets up in Melchett her parents are abroad and this morning she's going to Amirim Street, and already her head is fit to burst. Dubi rang to say that Giggy says that his father has wrangled us some finance, seed money to make the film, not in cash just an undertaking to top up an investment on condition we prove and on condition this and on condition that and also on condition that we sign up a director who has to be pretty well known, and we have to sign (my head my head) you and we have to sign, and we have to prove sources of finance authenticated by a registered accountant and Dubi says that Giggy made it a condition that he and his father should be kept in the picture and that he, that is Dubi, would open a special account, the Nirit account, and he would deposit such and such a sum at once and in the next phase Giggy's source would inject an equivalent sum and not a cent would leave the account without both their signatures, that is Dubi and Giggy, not you, not you, you're not investing a penny, on the contrary, we are purchasing the copyright from you, we is Dubi and Giggy, and you will get a token sum now and so much percent if it works out. In addition we have to sign up at least two guarantors. Get up girl drink some coffee take an aspirin and go to Bat Yam (my head my head) to sign this paper to sign only if Albert lets me, only if he assures me that the paper is OK. And Giggy will come and Dombrov as well and Bettine too for sure and maybe a lawyer. Albert will serve tea and savory sticks, Bettine will get up to help him but I'll stop her with a look. I'll go to the kitchen and she won't dare follow she'll just burn me up with that voodoo stare that she picked up from some old Greek who calls up the dead and fucks up the living. Now who's going to lend me two hundred shekels. Get moving Nirit go to Bat Yam.

How would I like to write?

Like an old Greek who calls up the dead and shakes up the living. Or like
a snowman passing alone and barefoot. To record the mountain to note
the sea with a fine tip, like sketching out a pattern for embroidery.
To write like a Russian travelling merchant making his way from here
to China. He finds a shack. And sketches it. In the evening he looks,
in the night he draws, and he finishes before dawn. Then he pays and
goes on his way with the break of day.

With or without

Like an open fracture like a broken bone sticking out of the torn flesh, my mother rises in the night from the shadow on the ceiling, saying to me Amek it's two o'clock why aren't you asleep and why are you smoking again. Go to the kitchen child drink some warm milk then get back into bed and sleep. Don't think about me in the night I am insomnia think instead about foggy rain in the forest and a fox seeking shelter among fir trees in the dark and it will lull you to sleep. In the dark among the fir trees Old Somnia walks with a wet headscarf sodden dress soaked to the skin a crooked stick in her shrivelled hand a weary witch named Somnia roams in the dark in the rain lost in the foggy trees shuffling from shadow to shadow wandering away from me out there yet passing through me on her way, backwards and forwards, criss-crossing me like a valley that she has turned from a valley into a vale of tears with her sleepless wandering. Maybe all this is just because I have left some door flapping.

Dita offers

Give me five minutes to try to sort out this screwed-up business. People are
constantly being ditched. Here in Greater Tel Aviv for example I bet
the daily total of ditchings is not far short of the figure for burglaries.
In New York the statistics must be even higher. Your mother killed herself
and left you quite shattered. And haven't you yourself ditched any number
of women? Who in turn had ditched whomever they ditched in favor of you,
and those ditched guys had certainly left some wounded Ditchinka lying
on the battlefield. It's all a chain reaction. OK, I'm not saying, I admit
being ditched by your own parents is different, it bleeds longer.
Specially a mother. And you an only son. But for how long? Your whole life?
The way I see it being in mourning for your mother for forty-five years is
pretty ridiculous. It's more than ridiculous: it's insulting to other women.
Your wife, for instance. Or your daughters. I find it a turn-off myself.
Why don't you try and see it my way for a moment: I'm twenty-six and you'll
soon be sixty, a middle-aged orphan who goes knocking on women's doors
and guess what he's come to beg for. The fact that before my parents
were even born your mother called you Amek isn't a life sentence. It's
high time you gave her the push. Just the way she chucked you. Let her
wander round her forests at night without you. Let her find herself
some other sucker. It's true it's not easy to ditch your own mother, so why
don't you stick her in some other scene, not in a forest, let's say in a lake:
cast her as the Loch Ness monster, which as everyone knows may be
down there or may not exist, but one thing is certain, whatever you see or
think you see on the surface isn't the monster, it's just a hoax or an illusion.

But how

Ditch her, you say, it's easy for you to say it,
bail out like a fighter pilot ditching a plane
that's in a spin or on fire. But how can you jump from a plane
that's already crashed and rusted or sunk under the waves?

From out there, from one of the islands

This morning outside her window Bettine Carmel sees
grey rain, shutters, washtubs, puddles in a deserted backyard.
Between kitchen balconies bare clotheslines are strung.
Ugliness and beauty, Bettine reflects, both attest, or at least point,
to the existence of some invisible presence, a silent, awesome
presence of which they bring us neither the voice nor the echo
but only a shadow of a shadow. Where is the boat, Bettine?
Where are those islands you mentioned? Here there is only
a peeling back wall. Rusty shutters. Tin roofs. And rain
pouring down not in torrents but splat, splat: like pus. A bus
bursts puddles and throws up mud like a whale's spout.
Where are those islands, Bettine? When do we sail?
And where to? Avram's old toilet things have been standing
next to the basin in your bathroom for twenty-one years,
a stiffened shaving brush, a dried shaving stick and a blunt
razor, and out there among the garbage cans in the yard in all that rain
a wet cat writhes, wailing hoarsely with tormented desire.
Those islands you mentioned, Bettine, when you asked me
if I believed in them, the Invisible Carmel, a silent awesome
presence, instead of replying yes or no I cracked a joke. I
tossed you some vapid witticism because then, when you asked me,
I was simply not all there. There was no me at home in my head.
Now that I'm back in residence there is no need to ask me
if I believe or disbelieve in those islands because as of this moment
those islands are me and from out there, from one of the islands,
I am calling to you through the rain, You come too, Bettine.

There is definitely every reason to hope

Bettine, you come too. There's a meeting at Amirim Street about *Nirit's Love*, tea and coffee are being sipped, savory sticks nibbled. Dombrov is full of words and Giggy Ben-Gal is picking his teeth. In a brass lamp in the shape of a pomegranate all four bulbs are lit because the day is gloomy. The new contract looks fair, but still Bettine rewords a clause, for the sake of clarity, and Albert raises three questions and suggests a couple of minor changes. Absalom in his head, Absalom, my son my son. In Bengal now it's five o'clock; on the radio they said the Brahmaputra has flooded. Stay clear of the water, my son. Keep away from low-lying areas. As for the Narrator, he is having a whispered conversation with Dita at one end of the sofa, the script lying across their laps. (Albert phoned him in Arad and asked him to read it, to give his opinion, to come, if he could, to the meeting.) Two hundred yards from here, the sea is having a whispered conversation with the sea, not cracking jokes but trying on silver baubles, taking them off, putting them on, polishing them, replacing emerald with lead. On the chair where Nadia used to sit is a pile of coats, scarves, we were all afraid it would rain, so far it has held off but it still looks threatening. Seemingly lit from within, clouds are swept eastward to the mountains and on toward Bengal. There, in the center of Dacca, in a corner of Café Mondial, Rico is waiting for two of the Dutchmen whom he arranged to meet up with here when he last saw them in Tibet. How is he to know that they've been in the Hague since the day before yesterday? This coffee table, the chairs, the armchair, the sideboard, were all made by Elimelech the carpenter some twenty years ago for a song because he and Albert both came from Sarajevo, they were vaguely related and had been school friends. Albert checked the carpenter's accounts every year and filled out his tax return. That is an old story, long since over. Giggy Ben-Gal now makes a suggestion: What this story needs, apart from

Nirit and her hermit who lives on the edge of a village, is another twist, like a one-night stand with an Arab farmhand, or let's say a little lesbian scene with a neighbor. Bettine suggests finishing with the bit where Nirit and the man are feeding the pigeons, because what comes afterward, the traveller, the dead fox, seems too morbid to her and overly symbolic. Dubi considers that the traveller definitely adds a deep mystical element to the ending. As for the Narrator, he recommends deleting several of the long silences which he regards as a bit of an affectation. Dita says nothing. Albert hesitantly apologizes and remarks that silences can actually sometimes express what words cannot. Meanwhile Bettine stands up, clears away the cups and plates, and stops on her way to the kitchen to open the curtains wide. The sight of the wintry sea which is now a virulent green makes her think that maybe this whole argument is unnecessary. Wrapped in the silence of empty spaces the brightly-lit earth floats from darkness to darkness. More tea? Or some coffee? No thanks—everyone has got things to do, promises to keep, business to see to, chores that can't be put off. Thank you. Must say goodbye and be off. It was nice, and as for the project, the script, it's in excellent hands. There is every reason to hope it will enjoy enormous success. We're off to a flying start.

Who cares

After that, in the car, the news. A soldier in the South Lebanon Army
has been fatally wounded and two Israelis slightly injured. In
Hazor in Galilee another small business has closed, its nine employees
are on hunger strike. A math teacher in Netanya has been
abusing his daughters for the past six years. A car went off the road
near Betar and ended up in a ravine: a father and mother and
their two sons; a daughter who survived is in a critical condition.
Epidemic and famine in Burundi. A woman in Holon has jumped.
The rain will continue. There is a warning of flooding
in low-lying areas. And a hurricane in the United States.
Who cares about *Nirit's Love*.

Little boy don't believe

In the summer of 1946 my mother and father rented a holiday room
in the flat of a tailor in Bat Yam. One night I was woken by a
coughing sound that was not coughing, and that was the first time in my life
that I heard a grown-up stranger crying through the wall. All
the darkness long he cried, and awake and frightened I lay still not to
disturb my parents until when the darkness was weaker I crept out and
saw him on the balcony his shoulders were shaking a bird flew up in the
silence of the dawn and the man pointed to it and said to me Little boy,
don't believe. Fifty years have gone by and the bird is no longer
or the man. Or my parents. Only the sea is still there
and even it has changed from deep blue
to grey. Little boy don't believe. Or do. Believe. Who cares.

Nadia hears

The bird wakes her. Lying on her back with her eyes shut, thinking
What's left apart from the place mat she's started and may still finish.
What's left is a wish that the pain will go away
that it will all go away and stop bending over her.
She lies as though she has left her launching pad and is now
moving along the Milky Way and already the planet
from which she was launched is far off, has shrunk till it can no longer be
distinguished from tens of thousands of other stars.
A bird on a branch calls to her and Nadia is lying
wiping away the good and the bad, like a woman who has nearly
finished washing the floor, walking backward toward the door, drawing
the mop toward her, all she has left to do is to wipe away the traces on
the wet floor of her own footprints. The pain is still sleeping: her hostile
body has not woken with her at the sound of the bird, with all its knives.
Even shame, her lifetime companion, has gone. It has ceased to gnaw at her.
Everything is letting go of her and Nadia is letting go of everything,
like a pear from a branch: the pear is not picked but a ripened pear drops.
Right now at four in the morning Nadia is the most alone she has ever been,
not alone like a sick woman hearing a bird in a garden but alone like a bird
with no garden no branch no wing. She lays her shrivelled hand on her
withered breast because suddenly for a moment the sound of the bird is
confused with a cry from a cradle at night, the baby's lips are open wide
to tickle her breast, or perhaps it is not her baby but a man covering it
with his palm, stroking it squeezing and soothing, slipping the nipple
between his lips describing with his tongue on her flesh
shivers that descend to the roots of her spine

and thus the needles of pain awake from their sleep and like
a small child in the dark she puts a finger in her mouth. *Narimi narimi*
has gone and now she needs an injection.

Half a letter to Albert

After the funeral I wrote a letter to Albert, half of it personal, which I do not
want to quote here, and the other half a kind of meditation, which I
shall reconstruct in other words. The desert and the sea, like you, insist on
balancing a joint bank account, evaporation, clouds, floods, the wind whirls
continually, rivers run into the sea, but there is no comfort in this:
from now on you are on your own without her among the heavy
brown furniture with embroidered mats lace curtains bellied for a moment by
the sea breeze which the next moment lets them hang slack. Whenever
I'm in town I'll try to drop in for a glass of tea. Try to be strong, Albert,
and phone me whenever you like. As for the assessments I sent you to check,
there's no hurry, it's not at all urgent.

The Narrator drops in for a glass of tea and Albert says to him

I read an article of yours, fire and brimstone, in yesterday's *Yediot*. Rico
showed it to me, he said, Read this, Dad, and don't get worked up,
just try to grasp where we are living and where all this lunacy is leading us.
That's what he said, more or less. I think he's even further to the left
than you, this repressive state and so on. I'm not so moral a person
as either of you, but I don't like the present situation much either.
Mostly I say nothing, from a deep-seated fear that in responding to
this or that wrong even I may come out with things that are not exactly
right. Anger sends out secondaries. Naturally I have every respect
for the brave child who shouts that the emperor is naked when the
crowd is cheering Long live the emperor. But the situation today is that the
crowd is yelling that the emperor is naked and maybe for that reason
the child ought to find something new to shout, or else he should
say what he has to say without shouting. As it is, there is so much
noise, even here, the whole country is full of screaming, incantations,
amulets, trumpets, fifes and drums. Or else the opposite, biting sarcasm:
everyone denouncing everyone else. Personally I'm of the opinion
that any criticism of public affairs ought to contain shall we say up to
twenty percent sarcasm, twenty percent pain, and sixty percent
clinical seriousness, otherwise everyone is mocking and jeering at each other,
everyone starts making false noises and everything is filled with malice.
Help yourself, have some of the other one, Nadia's sister-in-law baked them
for me so I'd have something to offer people who come to pay
their condolences. Try the cheesecake, whichever you like, they're both
very good. When you write for the papers, of course you must write
whatever you wish, even harsh things, but don't forget that the human
voice may have been created to express both protest and ridicule, but

essentially it contains a considerable percentage of quiet, precise speech
which is meant to come out in measured words. It may seem
that amid all the hubbub such a voice has no chance,
but nevertheless it's worth using it, even in a small room among three
or four listeners. There are still some people in this country who maintain
that the emperor is usually neither naked nor fully dressed, but, for example,
wearing clothes that do not suit him. He may even be excellently
dressed, but every bit as foolish as the cheering crowd, or the other
crowd that is no longer cheering, but jeering, or shouting that
the emperor is dead, or deserves to be. And anyway, who says that
a naked emperor is such a bad thing? After all, aren't the crowd also naked,
and the tailor and the little boy? Perhaps the best thing for you is to
steer clear of the procession altogether. Stay put in your house in Arad
and try to write in a quiet way if you can. At times like these, quiet
is the most precious commodity in the country. And let there be no
misunderstanding, I'm talking about quiet, definitely not about silence.

In Bangladesh in the rain Rico understands for a moment

With his back to his mother on the bridge in the warm rain
between a small town and a swamp Rico hears wet voices
in the distance. Women, foggy bears, are laughing in the flooded
field and one of them waves to him, inviting him to join them.
His waterlogged hair in his face and a whiff of stray smell
that reminds him of overripe figs, the smell of Dita with his
tongue in her ear and his hand stroking the inside of her thigh.
The warm rain keeps falling and under the bridge the muddy
river flows porridge-like. Sorrow and desire come, desire rises like
mercury in the thermometer of his cock pressed against the wall
of the bridge while his hands move to and fro over the rough
parapet. He looks at the trees with their roots half-exposed
in the soggy air, extra-terrestrial fingers, clutching at nothing.
Because his back is to his mother, inevitably he is facing
his father. If he turns his back on his father he will face
his mother again. He must change this staging, move my parents
closer to each other so that I can have my back to both
and return. The peasant woman who was calling him gives up
and stoops toward the mud, as the rain goes on and on.

Magnificat

Morning of orange-tinged joy: I get up at half past four and by five I have finished my coffee and am settling down at my desk, and almost at once there emerge two fully-formed lines running straight from my pen to the paper like a kitten weaving on tiptoe out of the bushes, there they are as though they were not written but always existed, not mine but their own. The light of the hills to the east cannot keep its hands to itself, shamelessly groping at private parts, causing heavy breathing all around, in birds branches and bees, so here we are delightedly leaving the desk and going off to work in the garden, although it is not even six, the fictional Narrator, the whole cast of characters, the implied author, the early-rising writer, and I.

Roses, myrtles, bougainvillaea, violets and sage have all gathered dewdrops and are now gently lit. Rico and Giggy Ben-Gal are clearing the ground round the two lemon trees, while Nadia, my father and Dombrov are pruning suckers from the roses and Avram is helping the author and Albert to hoe the edges of the flowerbed, weeding by hand among the flowers. Bettine, my mother and Dita are stooping and tying sweet peas to canes and even the Russian merchant stops on his way to China, and repairs the vine trellis, while my daughter Fania helps him, asking him how much they know in Nanking about Nizhni and how Nizhni looks from Nanking, and Maria is planting a window box and here are the Dutchmen as well, Thomas Johan Wim and Paul, making holes in the ground where Elimelech the carpenter tells them to, and my daughter Galia is pruning even though she would definitely have laid the whole thing out quite differently, and the man who was Nadia's first husband hums as he rakes up dead leaves and my son Daniel turns over the soil, improvising tunes with the fork, and the carpenter's daughter follows him with a roller, while Rajeb spreads fertilizer. In Sea Road

and in Cyclamen Street my little grandchildren, Dean, Nadav, Alon and Ya'el,
are still dreaming, while here in the garden, careful not to wake them, I caress
the sweet air that trembles around their hair, suppressing a powerful urge
to lick their cheeks or foreheads, to nibble their toes with my teeth.
Morning of orange-tinged joy, every wish is switched off and only delight
is alight. Grief fear and shame are as far from me today as one dream is
from another. I take off my shoes, play the hose on my feet my plants and
the light, whatever I have lost I forget, whatever has hurt me has faded,
whatever I have given up on I have given up on, whatever I am left with
will do. My children's thirty fingers, my grandchildren's forty, and my garden,
and my body, the few lines that came right this morning, and here at the window
my lovely wife who is close to the core of life is calling us all indoors, there is
bread ready sliced cheese and olives and salad, and soon there'll be coffee
as well. Later I'll go back to my desk and maybe I'll manage to bring back
the young man who went off to the mountains to seek the sea
that was there all the time right outside his own home. We have wandered
enough. It is time to make peace.

Where am I

Why do we never see you anywhere, they say to him, why
do you bury yourself in that hole, they say, far away from your friends,
with no parties, no nights out, no fun, you ought to get out,
see people, clock in, show your face, at least give some signs
of life. Forget it, he says to them, I get up at five o'clock have a coffee
and by the time I have erased and written six or seven lines
the day's already over and evening is falling to erase.

Bettine is at home again tonight. She has drawn the curtains and rolled down the blinds to the balcony so as not to have to see the fat neighbor opposite excavating his nose, hairy in an undershirt and sweat pants gawking from his armchair at some sitcom on the television. On the other side the sea, smooth tonight, chilly, shining darkly, a sea like the black glass nameplate of a respectable firm, with lines of gleaming gold writing, a pricey, highly polished sea, Current Liquidations Ltd. Bettine is in her armchair, lit by the glow from a parchment lamp shade, reading Troyat's biography of Chekhov. At the end of each page she shuts her eyes and thinks about the Narrator, he must be in Arad in the desert now, at the desk that Elimelech the carpenter made for him. She dips a honey cake into the tea that has gone cold in the cup at her side: on the cover is a photograph of Dr. Chekhov, almost a young man but his soft beard and hair and eyebrows are turning silver. He is wearing a striped jacket with wide lapels and a waistcoat, a stiff collar with a bow tie that is slightly askew, and a sad pince-nez secured by a cord. His eyes are those of a humble doctor who has made his diagnosis and knows what is going to happen but has not told his patient yet, although he knows that it is his duty to tell him now. I'm not the Almighty, his eyes say to the patient in front of him, after all you've known for some time now deep down inside, although you hoped, I hoped too, that these tests would surprise us and announce a reprieve. I cannot grant a reprieve, say Dr. Chekhov's eyes in the photograph, but I can and must do something now to block the pain. I'll prescribe you some tincture of opium. I'll also give you a sleeping potion, and some morphine injections to help you breathe. Get plenty of fresh air, sunshine and rest, don't try to do anything, just wrap up warm and sit in a wicker chair in the garden in the shade of the arbor and dream. Our business here is grim and hopeless, it goes round and round in circles, it is dreary and troublesome, but I'll prescribe you a dream and delusion, that you will still recover, that you will drive in your carriage to Tula, to Kazan, that you will still send rafts laden with merchandise down the river, that you will still buy Nikitin's estate at a favorable price, that you will still charm Tania Fyodorovna into leaving that vulgar Gomilev and coming back to you. Sit and dream. Dr. Chekhov is lying, and the shadow of a humble smile flits around the corners of his mouth. My soul is weary, he writes to Suvorin in August 1892, "I am bored. Not my own master, thinking about nothing but diarrhea, waking suddenly at night at the bark of a dog or a knock at the gate, are they coming to call for you? Travelling in a trap drawn by a worn-out mare along unknown tracks, reading about nothing but cholera, waiting for nothing but its coming, and at the same time feeling totally indifferent to the illness and the people you are treating." And in another letter: "The peasants are coarse, filthy, suspicious, I am the most wretched of the doctors in the district, my carriage and horse are useless, I do not know the roads, I can't see anything at night, I have no money. I tire very quickly, and above all I cannot forget that I must write, and I have a mighty urge to spit on the cholera and sit down and write." Bettine lays the book face down open on the arm of her chair and goes to the kitchen to put the kettle on for tea. Through her kitchen window the fat neighbor in his kitchen window opposite, in a long-sleeved vest and sweat pants, leans staring into the darkness or peering into her window, is caught out and smiles guiltily, perhaps he is dreaming about sending rafts down the river. Bettine draws the curtain and shuts him out. It's a quarter to eleven, the Narrator is still up, she dials. Sorry to call so late. I just wanted to tell you that Dita has moved back to Albert's because she has lent the flat he rented for her in Mazeh Street to Dombrov, who has been evicted from his own flat because he owes rent, and Giggy Ben-Gal, who promised to advance him some cash on account, has gone off to Spain and forgotten. And there was a postcard yesterday from Bengal, he's still chasing his shadow, as usual. Do you happen to have read Troyat's book about Chekhov? It brings me, right here in Bat Yam, a sense of fallen leaves in the snow, a sense of vast gardens abandoned to the autumn wind. It's all quite hopeless really, but at the same time quite diverting. It turns out that something that never was and never will be is all that we have. We are woken suddenly at night, every time a dog barks or a gate creaks, but the barking subsides to a whimper, the gate stops creaking, and all is quiet again. Did I interrupt you while you were writing? I'm sorry. Good night. By the way, next time you're in Tel Aviv call me, we'll have a glass of tea at my place or on Albert's veranda. It wasn't bad, what you wrote about the sea tonight, a pricey sea, smooth black with golden letters, a respectable company, Current Liquidations Ltd. Spit on the cholera. Just sit down and get on with your writing.

In a remote fishing village in the south of Sri Lanka Maria asks Rico

A virgin? A waitress? A nun? What shall I be tonight? Only not
your mother again. But first of all play the flute. Not in here. Let's
go down to the beach; there you can play for me and tell me
a story. One by one the fishing boats are taking to the sea
in a shimmer of lamps, licking the waves with their oars,
like tongues on a breast. Maria is in a wind-swollen skirt, he
is barefoot in jeans and a T-shirt, walking not by her side
but a few steps behind her. Whenever he played he drew
to him animals, bushes, meadows, mountains bent over
to hear, streams left their beds, the north wind froze not to miss
a note, the birds fell silent, even the sirens stopped singing
and listened. When his beloved died he followed her down
to the underworld, charmed Persephone with his playing,
from the eyes of Death himself he wrung five or six iron tears,
and he hypnotized his dog. Surely every poet every musician
every charlatan tries like him to bring back the dead. The one condition
was that he not turn back or look behind, that he
walk ahead without turning around. On the face of it this
was an easy condition, an obvious security measure, to protect
the privacy of the underworld. Hades, however, that iron-teared
rhymester, knew his victim's mind: the wise man's eyes may be
in his head, but not so the poet's. A poet's eyes are in the back
of his neck. The minstrel always plays facing backward.
And so, as black turned to grey, his arms were drawn to embrace her
but she was no longer there. To play or to touch. Either or.
Since then he has been a wanderer and a fugitive like the young David
in the caves of Adullam, playing to the forests that froze to

hear his notes, playing to the hills. Try to imagine it Maria:
the rivers of sounds that have traversed the world since then,
including thunders, screams, barks, melodies, pleas, coughs,
shots, whispers, flutterings, the sighing of trillions of leaves,
earthquakes, drips, chirps, confessions, echoes and ripples of
echoes, all the innumerable sounds that, like everlasting autumn,
have long since buried the trickle of his piping. The winter
of the scuds, that I told you about in Bengal, Dita and I went together
to the old cemetery in a kibbutz called Ayyelet Hashahar, where
you can sometimes hear a sort of sound that promises you tonight
whatever you want on condition that you don't look back.

His father rebukes him again and also pleads a little

Listen carefully. This is your father speaking. A simple man,
a rather grey man, and so on and so forth, but still your father. The only one
you have, and that's something your irony can't change.
That cheap woman you're with may let off
fireworks in bed, I'm not an expert in such matters
and I'm sorry to mention it, but fireworks
go out and time is drying up and the summer is over and you are
not back. The summer is over the autumn is gone and what about you,
where are you? Shrouded in fog in limbo in the arms
of a whore. It's lucky your mother—well, never mind. Don't hang up.
Just a minute. Listen to me: Dita is back here. In your room.
Sometimes, just in my mind's eye, I look at her and think,
my grandchild is drying up. Wait. Don't put the phone down. The autumn
is over and you are just mist. Last night I dreamed of my own father,
he was kneading dough, grunting hoarsely in Ladino, *Stupido Albert,
asno*, in ten more minutes *se hizo hamets*. This call
is already costing me a fortune, but there's one more thing I have to tell you:
under the same roof she is waiting and so am I. There is something not right
about this. The summer is over and the autumn is gone; the rain brings me
a smell of dust. Don't come back too late.

In between

Like a sooty engine at the end of its journey the lit half
of the earth drags wearily toward the shadow
while the dark half gropes at the first line of light.

Dita whispers

My hand in the hay of your old chest
plucks straw
to line our nest

But Albert stops her

Her hand so light in the hay of my chest. On the back
of her hand my shrivelled hand. She's on my own. I'm on her own.
On my veranda. We are alone. The sea has taken, the sea
has given. A slim silhouette and a little shadow. A timid
shadow. That turns. Escapes. The sea gives and the sea
takes.

Then, in the kitchen, Albert and Dita

She is making an omelette, he is chopping a salad, her shoulder brushes
the skin of his arm like lips touching a lace veil. A cup drops. It doesn't break.
He takes this as a favorable omen: salad with olives, a big omelette,
yoghurt with honey and fresh strong black bread with ewes' milk cheese.
All this at nearly two o'clock at night, in Sri Lanka it's already morning
while here there's the smell of the kitchen after a meal. They clear away
the dishes, he'll wash up tomorrow, right now it's late. In the bathroom
the two of them: he in grey flannel pyjamas, she with a T-shirt down
to her thighs, he with his back to her, facing the bowl, she facing
the mirror, brushing her teeth, he's in his slippers, her feet are bare,
before going to sleep he wants to sew a button on for her,
on the side, on the waist of her orange skirt that he takes on his arm
to his room like a bride to her wedding bed. Close and breathing, close and
chilly, beyond his window the sea sighs. The doors are locked. Soon the bird

Scorched earth

The teeth of time, smoke without fire. On the back of my hand
I see the brown mark that once used to be, at the very same spot,
on my father's gnarled hand. And so my father is back
from underground. For years he has failed and now, at last,
remembered to hand over to his son a patch of pigment
from his estate. The teeth of time. Scorch-mark without fire.
Ancestral seal. The gift of the dead
on the back of your hand.

Good, bad, good

Maria can also read fortunes. She reads them in coffee grounds,
she puts on her glasses to read, Maria is not so young any more. There's
good news and bad news in the coffee. The bad news is that time
flies. The good news is that time heals. That the evening is fine.
The bad news, that we're out of coffee. And almost out of money.
Look, there's a goat, staring at us like a widow,
maybe she's mistaken us for a mother and son, never mind,
let her live with her mistake, after all, why should we argue with a goat?
Especially a goat who's a widow. Tonight we'll eat dates, we'll sleep on this
straw, and not shoo her away. Come here, touch me. Tomorrow Chandartal.

Dubi Dombrov tries to express

Twenty to three in the morning. This is the time, not six, that ought to be at the bottom of a clock: the lowest time, when you can see what's going to happen. Dubi Dombrov calls Dita Inbar who is napping over the *City News* behind the hotel reception desk, her cheek resting on her hand; by her side, in a plastic cup, some lemonade is losing the last of its fizz. Sorry, he says, I just thought you might be free now to chat a bit. I suddenly had this idea that if you could manage to touch your old man, say, or some other old man, for nine thousand dollars or so, it would put me in the clear, as they say. We could spread our wings and make one hell of a film. With money like that I'd even give you a fifty-fifty share of Dombrov Productions Ltd. We'll repay the money within a year. We won't just repay it, we'll double it. Two people who count, top people at Channel 2, have read the revised script and definitely see potential in it. The problem is that I'm a bit in the red. I've sold the Fiat (with nine parking tickets and only two days left on the insurance) but don't worry, I'll clear out of your flat in Mazeh Street the moment I get the money Giggy promised. Besides which I've got eczema, besides which I missed two months of my alimony and today I got a sequestration order in the mail plus a call-up for the reserves, twelve days in Kastina, besides which I haven't moved my bowels for three days. Excuse the details. If the old man won't chip in nine thousand maybe he could make it two, or even a grand? I've got a painting by Tumarkin that must be worth twice that, I'll make it a gift to you. Anyway, I've been wanting to give you something personal, something beautiful for some time. It's a rather repulsive picture, actually, but it's all I've got, Dita. Nobody can give what he hasn't got. I'm not asking anything from you Dita, only that you should try to see me in a slightly different light sometimes. If you can. As for the money, get as much as you can, the old man is wild about you, and you'll see that our film will take off after all. Even a couple of grand would do for starters, after that you'll be amazed how this venture of ours will run all by itself. Believe me,

I wouldn't for the life of me ask you for a penny if I had any choice. Tell me, Dita says, have you any idea what time it is? And tell me, Dita says, where are you living, anyway. To which Dubi Dombrov replies, with his bad breath hitting her across the switchboard and the wire, You want the truth? We're living in a flash. All of us. In a flash—it describes time and in a way it also describes space too. Honest, I wish I could put my body into storage, or mortgage it. I don't care if I don't get a cent for it. I'd even pay. All my troubles come from this lump of flesh that's clung to me since I was a child and doesn't let me rise above it. Nothing good ever came from it. It guzzles fuel like crazy and all it ever does is make me blush or squirm. This body of mine is forever flat on its face. If only I could get around town without it everything would be so easy. I'd stage a project the likes of which this city has never seen before. I'd be free from sleeping and breathing and smoking, no belly, no reserve duty, no debts, no fear of AIDS, I wouldn't give a shit. For all I care the Scuds can come again and take it off my back. Or I'll sell it to an organ bank or even donate it to a forensic lab or a transplant center, and then I'd go off to the beach as free as the air. And take it easy. Or I'd go further, Tibet, Goa, I could take your boyfriend's place and send him back to you, even though really I don't believe all this shit, that he's hanging out there with some Portuguese chick, his own private fado singer, some kind of sexy hot-gospeller, that whole business is just a load of bullshit, he's probably blowing his mind in some hole in India and the whole Maria thing is all in the Narrator's head, and he's the one you should really talk to, if you just fluttered your eyelashes at him and got him to make a couple of phone calls to the right people, he must know them all, then our film would be halfway to being made. Even that Giggy of yours is just a load of bullshit when it comes to it, and so am I, even more so. The real reason I called you at 3 a.m. is that I thought it was the only way I'd finally have the guts to express my feelings, and look what came out instead: a lump of shit. What time do you finish your shift? I'll wait for you outside the hotel, OK? Or perhaps I won't. What's the use.

Scherzo

He's fond of cheese, he chops salads fine,
no mortal man can chop them finer. Better a live
dog who this morning sent a thousand dollars to his son and to Dita
wrote a check for the sum of NIS 3,500. He's discontinued
his savings plan even though he knows the money's going down the tube.
Now he's reading *Yediot* and discovering that the state of the country
is also going from bad to worse. The magnates are arrogant,
peacock for foreign affairs, peacock for home affairs, little foxes
with high-falutin words. Dispensing a poor man's wisdom: tax adviser to
a greengrocer, an air-conditioning installer, he screws up his brown
face in the mirror like a raisin. To himself he says: The days
are going by. Yes sir, they are. The days are going by. I'm sorry
sir, excuse me sir, we're just about
to close. So sit down and finish going through these accounts. Try at least
to clear your desk. The newspaper can wait. Afterward, if there's time
you can change your shirt and go over to Bettine's. Go over there, stay
a while, chat, come home. Whatever you do it's no use.

Mother craft

Bettine, how are you? It's Dita. I'm calling to ask if by any chance
you've got his glasses? The dark ones? In the black case? No? Oh well,
we'll keep looking then. They must be here somewhere. Are you coming
over this evening? I'm working nights: I leave here at seven to be
at the hotel by eight. Do come. You can both have supper and sit outside
and chat on the veranda, only don't switch the light on, the mosquitoes
are hellish. You told me last winter that I make him needlessly sad,
or give him pointless needs, or something like that. I don't remember
exactly. Now I feel like telling you you shouldn't worry, Bettine.
There are no casualties. On the contrary: we both seem to be
definitely holding our own, if one can say that, and that's
how it is Bettine. I saw a big story in the paper today with pictures,
anxious moments in space, searching for the mother craft, is it or
isn't it out of control, I think something like that happens to lots
of people almost every day: finding losing finding again and
gasping for air. How on earth did we get here? It doesn't matter. If you
do happen to find his glasses will you bring them with you
when you come this evening. Even if you don't find them, come anyway.
It's better for the two of you to spend the evening together
than alone. And don't bring loads of stuff with you: I've
done plenty of shopping, the fridge is full.

It's me

Now it's me. I used to be Nadia and now
I'm not a spirit or a reincarnation or a ghost. Now
I'm the air my son breathes in his sleep on the straw,
I'm the sleep of the woman who's resting her head
on his shoulder. I'm also the sleep of my husband
who's fallen asleep on the living room couch
I'm my daughter-in-law's dream, her head in her hands
on the hotel desk I'm the swish of the curtain
that the sea stirs through the window. That's me.
I am all of their sleep.

A tale from before the last elections

A Knesset Member, Pessach Kedem, from Kibbutz Yikhat, found himself
left off the party list because of an intrigue, because some
cunning son-of-a-bitch grabbed his safe place near the top of the list.
Recovering from the shock and indignation he looked for a place, even
not a safe one, to hide his face in shame, a place secure from pitying
or gloating looks. At last, they say, his confidants managed to find him
a temporary billet as managing director or just company secretary
of some private ravine in the Tortoiseshell Range, down in the desert
not far from Arad. That's where the man now sits making notes,
remembering, fuming, scheming, growing armor, hiding his head,
retracting his limbs, burying his face in his armored plates, reviewing
the situation, transforming himself from an MK into a tortoise. And how
about you? Do you feel you are safe and secure near the top of the list?

Half-remembering, you have forgotten

Meanwhile he is working as a night watchman in a run-down refrigeration plant belonging to a Belgian fishery company in the Gulf of Kirindi, beneath a curtain of dark hills. Maria has moved on. Beyond those hills there is a steamy primeval jungle sweat-soaked with unceasing rains where there are monkeys, parrots, bats and huge snakes. *Aus Israel,* the Austrian engineer leered with a conspiratorial wink, *ach so,* in that case he certainly won't fall asleep on the job or just sit there gaping if a light flashes on the control panel. His wage, in Sri Lankan rupees, is three and a half dollars plus a fish he can grill on the embers after midnight, and each morning when he leaves he can take two fish fresh from the boats. His broom closet at the inn costs less than a dollar a day, and he spends a similar sum on rice, vegetables, a rented mosquito net, postcards and stamps. Meanwhile there's a boy, an abandoned child, whom he inherited from the previous watchman (who got him from his own predecessor), a quick-moving, shadowy creature, who somehow belongs to the fishery, he sleeps by day in some disused cooling compartment and at night among bearded pipes sticky with solidified engine oil, living the life of a little fish thief or honorary assistant night watchman. In and out of the dark gaps between refrigerators he slinks wolfishly, barefoot, he is six or possibly eight, he is in tatters, every night he is reborn after midnight, out of the shadows at the smell of grilled fish, an old rag round his loins, timidly sniffing he cleverly overtakes his own shadow and penetrates the circle of the watchman's fire, panting, his skin quivering to escape. In vain you attempt in English sprinkled with crumbs of Sinhalese, Come child here don't be afraid: he's been abused by other watchmen, before you, who seduced him with their smell of fish, and did one thing and another. Now he's more careful: give me first. Just throw him a tidbit of fish and he leaps, catches it in his teeth in mid-flight, retreats with his spoils to the shadows, then reappears to flicker around the ring of the fire, his pupils reducing the flames

to embers, his face in the half-light angelic but impure, a sly dishonest angel
well versed in gradations of winks, experienced in this and that: the previous
watchmen had done one thing and another, and another, but always he
had managed to float up to the surface of the swamp, velvety, girlish, unsullied,
with just a cunning-cautious spark in his eye. Night by night you throw
the tidbits less and less far, till at last he dares to snatch one from your hand
and flee. Or thus: you hold the fish just a little bit higher than he can jump,
till he tells you his name, where he lives, who his parents are. He doesn't
know. Nowhere. Never had any. So whose is he then? In guttural English,
with the Sinhalese trill: *Yourr honorr's sirr.* And a bow. As he speaks he leaps and
snatches the fish, sweet potato, or rice, with three swift hands. His voice
is warm and brown, like the smell of roast chestnuts. Within a few nights
he is climbing up of his own accord to nestle in your lap while skillfully
caressing you in one way and another, and also another, until you spot
what he's up to and stop him and carry him in your arms to your mattress
(submissive, pitiful, experienced, lying on his tummy for you). You cover
him with a sheet of greasy canvas, but he looks up at you with surprise, before
falling asleep all at once. You lay one hand on his forehead and the other
on your own, as though you were your mother. Soft and tired like the child
your head drops on your chest and the darkness draws out of you the hum
of a Bulgarian children's song without words, or with words you've forgotten,
half-remembering you have forgotten, but like the corpse of a drowned man
you can make out the shape of what you've forgotten. Toward dawn
you open your eyes, you're alone on the mattress, the child
has vanished without a trace, in the window silhouettes of boats
coming up from the seabed of night, all around the derelict plant mangy dogs
are barking, skinny dogs shrieking then sinking to a whimper, as a murky sun
chokes through the screen of haze: an opaque sunrise that resembles
a diseased, inflamed eye. Take a few fish and go to your bed. It's so hot.

It will come

It will come like a cat before evening. Soft and quick it will come.
Drowsy-cruel, sharp and light, it will come, silently,
on hovering paws, bow-taut back, furry, silky, evil,
crouching to spring it will come like a knife. Honing it will come. Its pupils
tiger-yellow, it is stealthy, arched, fawning, it will come like a cat
on a wall, lying in wait, patiently, coiled like a spring. It has seen a moth.
It won't give up.

Burning coals

It will come; it won't give up. Until it comes come back to me, don't
disappear, at least in the nights come back to me desire of women:
when I was a skinny pimply youth, day and night dreaming poems
dreaming women day and night you didn't leave me: with me
when I lay down, with me when I rose up, burning coals of my night
and shame of my day in my bed, at my school, in the street, in the fields,
scorched by desire for a woman but without a woman: a unicorn
in the morning in the daytime in the evening in my dreams, a brassière
hanging on a washing line, a pair of girls' sandals in the hall, a pencil
turning in the sharpener, a plump thick-braided girl soldier putting
a spoon full of sticky plum jam to her mouth, my blood thickened
to warm honey. Or in the evening, behind a curtain, the silhouette
of a woman combing another woman's hair, any rounded movement,
stirring, kneading, any sound descending to a whisper, a girl sewing
a button on her dress, the feel of face cream or soap, a rude joke,
a dirty word, a whiff of perfume mingled with a secret hint
of woman's sweat, fountained up scalding geyser,
surrounded with a vapour of shame. Even the word "woman" printed
or the curves of "breast" in cursive writing, or the sight of some
furniture on its back with its legs in the air made the stew
of my lust boil over and my body clench like a fist. Now an old male,
a unicorn of memories on his bed pleads with you to come back
to come back, desire of women, to come back to him at night,
give him back at least in a dream that trembling give back the scorch
of glowing coals, lest he forget you, lest he forget come what may come,
on hovering silken paws, soft, furry, yellow-eyed, comes sharp,
light and silent with sharp panther's fangs and a woman's curves.

Bettine tells Albert

Every weekend they bring the grandchildren to see me: the girl is a lamb
and the boy is a bear, she calls me Ranny Tee and he
pulls my hair. On Friday night they stay with me
and snuggle in my bed. I protect them
from the nightmares and the cold, and they protect me
from loneliness and death.

Never far from the tree

The apple never falls far from the tree. The tree stands
at the apple's bedside. The tree turns yellow and the apple turns brown
the tree sheds damp leaves. The leaves shroud
the apple. The cold wind leafs through them.
Winter comes autumn is over the tree is eaten the apple
rots. Very soon it will come. It will come it will hurt.

A postcard from Sri Lanka

Dear Dad and Dita, on the other side you can see three trees and a stone.
The stone is the grave of a girl called Irene, the daughter of Major Geoffrey
and Daphne Homer. Who were these Homers? Why did they come here?
What were they looking for? Nobody in the village can remember. Nobody
can explain either why they made a postcard out of it. Were they living here
or just passing through? I scraped the moss off the stone with my knife
and discovered that she died of malaria, at the age of twenty, in the summer
of 1896: more than a hundred years ago. Did her parents, that evening,
six hours before her death, still lie to her and say that she was getting better,
that in a couple of days she would be fully recovered? And what did she feel
when, between bouts of hallucination, she had a moment of lucidity, like a
hunted antelope, when she intercepted an exchange of glances and suddenly
realized that this was her death, that they had given up hope for her,
her parents and the doctor, that they were lying to her out of pity
and saying that the fever was abating and that by tomorrow
she would be better? Did she whisper That's enough, stop
pretending? Or did she feel sufficiently sorry for them to pretend right to
the end that she believed the lie that was tacitly contradicted by her mother's
weeping? And as she died convulsed by the light of a hurricane lamp
in the tent at four in the morning, who wiped the last beads of sweat from
her forehead? Who went outside first and who stayed with her a little longer
in the half-darkness of the tent? When morning came did Major Homer
force himself to shave? And did someone hand her mother a handkerchief
soaked in valerian? Because of the heat did they bury her that very morning
or did they wait till evening? And where and how did they travel on
from here? Did they leave at once? Or the next day? And how did the jungle
stand around the grave the first night after they left? A hundred years

have passed, so the pain has been stilled. Who is there to grieve? I wonder whether somewhere in the world there is still an old comb or nail file or mother-of-pearl brooch that belonged to that Irene. Perhaps in some drawer in an unused walnut dressing table, or a mouldy attic somewhere in Wiltshire? And who will want to keep her things, if any have survived? And what for? Only I, who have no photograph and no image of her, felt sad yesterday for that Irene. Just for a moment. Then it passed. I ate a grilled fish with some rice and fell asleep. Today everything is fine. Don't worry.

Albert blames

Haven't I told you a thousand times Nadia I beg you stop filling his head with such nonsense once and for all, he's still young and easily frightened, don't stuff him full of wolves and witches and snow, ghosts in the cellar and goblins in the forest. There aren't any forests or goblins here. We came to this country to put all that behind us, to live on yoghurt and salad with an omelette, to settle down, to change, to defend ourselves when we have no alternative, to banish the old troubles, to be cured of the ancient horror, to sit under the vine in the garden, to recover gradually from everything that happened before, and to begin to distinguish here at last between what is possible and what is sheer lunacy. Haven't I told you a thousand times that my son has to grow up to be a useful member of society, a decent, sensible man with no nonsense in his head in the clouds but with both feet planted firmly on the ground in this land where there are no cottages in the forest but only warm sand and housing schemes. That is what we have, I told you, and what we haven't got we must simply learn to do without. To draw a line. Now look what's happened because of you. You've filled his head with fairies and fog and you yourself have grown feathers and a beak and flown off into the cold. You've left me all these lace doilies and embroidered place mats, who needs them? We could have had a grandson by now. Or a granddaughter.

Like a well where you wait to hear

Toward evening the boy, who still called him Yourr Honorr, would whistle to drag him out of the dungeon of sweaty sleep, and the two of them would climb the hill to catch crickets, or go to the seashore to pick up seashells to sell. They saw *Superman* together twice at the Globe Cinema and when they came out they wrestled panting on the grass. He went to the store run by the man from Taiwan and from his meager savings he bought the child a pair of khaki shorts, some vests, sandals with soles made from tires, he ended up looking like a young scamp from Israel in the old days. Each evening he bought him a Coke, some dates, bubble gum, occasionally a sticky brown sweet made locally from coconut and honey. He taught him to play a game of marbles from Tel Aviv, and they also made a kite. At night, on duty, you used to grill him a fish over the fire and talk, and the boy would listen, and sometimes a sly look flickered across his face which showed for an instant that he was not always as angelic as he looked. In the mornings, for instance, when you were asleep would he curl up in a heap of rags in the disused refrigeration unit, or on a battered mattress in some shed, or would he go off somewhere else to collect what was due to him? One day you bought him a bubble pipe from the Taiwanese, and that is how you were seen, an angular, tousled young man in jeans and a T-shirt with a Hebrew slogan ("Let the animals live"), with a dark-skinned, rather feminine little boy, in a pair of new sandals and a kibbutz-style vest which had once been white, the two of you blowing bubbles. So what if some people were beginning to gossip, at the hostel, at the refrigeration plant. The philandering Austrian engineer slapped you in various places and leered, neighing *Ach so!* At the kiosk, when you had finished blowing bubbles, the boy learned from you the latest Tel Aviv slang. Then you bought two sticks of chewing gum and you sat chewing together on the stone opposite the petrol pump. Perhaps you should ask some passing tourist to take a Polaroid photo. And send it. In a letter. So they'd know. This child, listen, looks at you like a little abandoned monkey, not exactly looking you in the eye, more in the mouth, as though through your mouth he can see what's inside you. Besides which, he taught me a trick with a coin, the Devil only knows who taught it to him and what other things he knows without anyone knowing. He's like one of those lizards where if you pull off their tail they grow a new one, or more precisely like a well where you throw a stone in and wait to hear but you don't hear anything.

A negative answer

Question in a dream: and what was the fate of that well-mannered man, the draper who always knew what to say and what to pass over in silence? The man who was Nadia Danon's first husband? A scrubbed and scented, cheerful man, inclined to fixed habits, who sang Sabbath songs delightfully in a rich, resonant tenor voice. He may be living to this day in a suburb of Marseilles or Nice, pink-cheeked, flourishing, surrounded by charming widows. Or perhaps he is here in Israel, living in Kiryat Ono, a widower and pensioner, the treasurer of the House Committee, still hoping that one day his only daughter Rachel, a twice-divorced doctor of forty, will return from San Antonio or Toronto, marry a moderately observant Jew, open her own private clinic, and invite him to live with them, let's say in a modest little cabin at the end of their garden. To his question in a dream he receives a negative answer. She is there and you are here, totally on your own since the day Rex was run over. You have to get over your grief, put on a jacket and tie, pick up your carved cane, and go to the Animal Protection Society to choose yourself a new puppy despite everything, and start all over again. But it will be difficult to relate to a new puppy now: if you call him Rex he will remind you every day that Rex no longer exists, and if you call him Chief he won't help you forget anything. Better to give up dream questions and get on at last with finding a replacement for that refrigerator that rumbles like a heavy smoker and interrupts your sleep.

Abishag

It's cold tonight. And rainy.
His hands are so thin.
He's not really old
and I'm not in his arms.

His hands are so tender
clasped in my palms,
I'm changing a baby
born to me from his son.

He's really not old. Restless,
the sea outside in the dark
exhales. Thrashes. Gropes
the sandy beach with its waves.

As though changing his grandson
my hands encircle his.
For a moment he was a baby,
but now he's a father again.

He closes his eyes to keep watch

A small surprise party: the people who work at the Property Tax Board are saying goodbye tonight to an old colleague who has reached retirement age. So from eight to midnight Albert has offered to look after Bettine's grandchildren who are sleeping in her bed. On a shelf in her bedroom is a photo of her husband Avram, a distant relation of Nadia's, with a precisely trimmed grey moustache, and a beret on his head. A smell of talc and shampoo enfolds Bettine's habitual faint perfume. The little girl is fast asleep, clutching a sheep with a missing ear, from time to time in her sleep she takes a single deep breath. The boy is tossing and turning, he's worried, he fears the worst, he thinks there's a bear lurking in the corridor. In vain Albert carries him outside to see for himself that there's nothing there. He is frightened. He wants his mummy. He wants Granny 'Tine. He wants the light on. He asks Albert to turn off the dark, quick. In vain Albert sings a Serbian lullaby from his childhood in Sarajevo and another haunting song in Bulgarian with which Nadia used to lull Rico and herself to sleep. In vain. A faint light comes from the kitchen and a glimmer from a street lamp enters through the window, trembling slightly because of the sea breeze stirring in the chinaberry tree. Albert goes to the kitchen to warm a bottle that Nadia has prepared before she went out. Bettine, he corrects himself. But Nadia won't let go. He returns to the bedroom and finds the boy asleep. Now he goes down on his knees on the matting to pick up the animals, bricks, books, a xylophone missing two of its bars, stoops to lay a teddy bear by the boy's shoulder, covers both children with a blanket, sits down in Bettine's armchair, and closes his eyes to keep watch.

Xanadu

—till one evening he does not come to whistle, Wake up Yourr Honorr, let's
go get a Coke, and then let's go shrimping in the shallow rock pools in
the bay. First you scan the sky for the dragon kite you made him. Not there.
That night he does not pop out as usual from the shadows behind the pipes
and the smell of grilled fish.

Nor the next day.

He has disappeared.

In vain you go looking for him at the plant, in the cellars, on the shore, in
his disused refrigerator, to no avail you quiz the soft-drink seller
in the square or the Taiwanese storekeeper: vest khaki shorts a pair of
suspenders like an H? Always lugging a bag full of snails and Coca-Cola tops?
No use. So many children are abandoned here, cocksuckers, beggars,
pickpockets, who can tell them apart? The fishermen you question
this morning snicker, wink, what's the problem, find another one instead,
there's no shortage of his sort here. Has he been kidnapped? Got lost?
Drowned? Or found another uncle on the side? Only yesterday you washed
his hair; the boy bit, struggled, but came back in the evening with a gift for
you: a live jellyfish in a can of seawater. And the grief like a creeping stone:
the boy isn't here. He's gone. The boy who was here has gone. The boy
has gone. Lost. With his blue bag of snails and his sandals made from tires,
tied with a frayed string. A dustboy, so velvety, he found you rather odd,
what's the matter with you, a corrupt angel's smile, innocently seductive, pure
and smart, but suddenly a startled little monkey would cling and cuddle
in your arms, huddling and burrowing with a take-good-care-of-me.

You didn't. The boy has gone. The boy who was yours has gone. This
evening in the square three neon signs in Sinhalese and one in English:

Xanadu dance bar, first and last drink free on the house. Order a gin. Talk
for a while to one of those easy girls who by the way is also called Xanadu.
A boy. Lost. Not mine. Vanished. Don't know his name. He always calls me
Your Honor and I call him Come-Here. Eight. Or six. Who can tell?
So many children abandoned here. Maybe he needs help. He may be
screaming to me in the dark. Or no longer screaming. On the barbed wire
opposite is a torn scrap of kite. Another kite. Not ours. And warm rain
has been hanging for hours in the air. Sit and mourn. There's plenty of time.
Xanadu stays open till daylight.

If only they let her

At six in the evening Bettine is walking along the shadier sidewalk to Viterbo's pharmacy, a woman with attractive hips, wearing a skirt made of an Indian material, and earrings, with her hair bobbed, her handbag swinging from her shoulder. Two days ago she won six hundred shekels in the lottery, and she is going to spend the money on Albert as well as herself. Besides acamol and calcium tablets, she is going to buy essence of propolis and echinacea, ginseng, and capsules of garlic and zinc. On second thought she will also get some brewer's yeast and a jar of royal jelly for Dita who is looking washed-out, and two little toothbrushes and some vanilla-flavored toothpaste for her grandchildren on Friday evening. There's something cheap about that Dita, she's so caught up in herself, always preening, but she's rather touching too. The truth is it wouldn't hurt that bulldog Dubi Dombrov if someone took care of him. (Bettine casts a fleeting glance on his behalf toward a display of health care products but warns herself, Don't overdo it.) As she leaves the pharmacy at twenty past six, Mr. Viterbo follows her with a smile that has no ostensible cause yet is not groundless. Instead of heading straight for Albert's she walks, clutching her plastic bag, to the seaside esplanade from which one can see the sun moving fairly fast toward the sea which, for its part, receives its sharp stabs of simple color and responds with its own complex colors. If you stop talking sometimes, my teacher Zelda said to me when I was about seven, maybe things will sometimes be able to speak to you. Long afterward I found in a poem of hers "*a very faint quivering that moves the leaves when they meet the light of the dawn.*" Bettine is a far less thin-skinned mortal than my teacher Zelda, but something sometimes reminds me of her, for instance the way Bettine says, Listen, here's what I saw, or, Now don't you repeat that. A few days ago she said to me, Try to visualize what is implied in the bureaucratic expression "expired" that we use ten times a day without hearing what it is actually saying, but if you stop to think about it there is good reason to be startled. In my dream I am still in the pharmacy where I've been sent to return something embarrassing, like a bra or a garter belt from her clothesline that has somehow ended up at our place by mistake, and I try to give it back but she argues with me, Take a boy like Giggy, take someone like Dombrov even, and I say to her, I have taken them, and she smiles, not at me but at the pharmacist Viterbo, who smiles with her against me as he wraps a mouth organ for me which I haven't bought. Dear Bettine (I say to her in the dream as though I am greeting her at some formal occasion), why don't you bring your grandchildren over to our place this week-end, to play with our grandchildren? It won't fuse together, she says, and I am amazed in my dream and suddenly I'm not at the pharmacy but running across a plot of wasteland as the sirens howl. Little boy don't believe. Or do. Believe. What then. An invisible presence, she says, a terrible mute presence, and every-thing, from a stone to an urge, brings us not its sound, or an echo of its sound, but only a shadow of a shadow of a shadow or maybe not even that, but only a trembling, only a longing for shadow. Such is Bettine's creed, such is her faith. One evening in the summer she called me in Arad to chat about some book she was reading, and she told me she thought it was all quite hopeless really but at the same time quite amusing, because it turns out that something that never was and never will be is all that we have and that is what she wants to fuse to-gether. Dear Bettine. If only they would let you.

The winter is ending

In south Bat Yam they're building a new mall, they've closed a grocery shop
and opened a fashion boutique or a bank, dedicated a garden to Yitzhak
Rabin, with a fountain and benches. In Bangladesh there has been more
flooding: the monsoon has washed away bridges, villages and crops. Not here.
Here we are expecting primaries, scuds or devaluation, whichever comes first.
Ben-Gal & Partners have purchased a new plot to build luxury apartments
and duplexes and commissioned a ninety-second promotional film from
Dubi Dombrov: your dream home, penthouse with sea view. Dita Inbar
wrote the script. Apart from that, she's been to the hairdresser's, and bought
a spring dress and sandals. She is writing another screenplay
about the eccentric Greek in Jaffa who brought the dead back for
a short while, before he died himself. Then his heirs quarrelled about his flat.
Instead of a lawsuit, for a modest fee, Albert Danon has worked out a
compromise. On Tuesday Bettine is giving him supper, on Thursday night
she is coming round for tea and cakes on the veranda. The winter is ending.
The birds are at work. This light is pleasant and the nights are quiet.

A sound

Now everything is closed in Bat Yam except the duty pharmacy, where
a cool neon light is flickering. Behind the counter, in a white coat, sits
an Italian Jew, no longer young, who for three hours has been reading
line by line everything written in the daily paper, which while he reads
has become yesterday's paper. He wonders aloud but he knows that
there will be no answer. From the pocket of his white coat he takes
a pen and taps the side of his empty cup four or five times. It is not the
sound that startles him but the renewed silence: now it is really pure.

He's gone

For ever. He's gone. And from now on
it will hurt. Get up. Go. To bed. Or
not. Sit down. Have another gin
or don't. Go out. Come back. He's
not. Only there, on the rumpled canvas,
a cigarette-butt of his smell is left
among the brew of fish smells.

All there

The sky is dark and empty. A mist flows through a mist.
It has not rained this evening. It seems it will not rain.

It's grey and calm here. Getting darker. A still bird on a post.
Two cypresses grow almost joined. A third one grows apart.

I'm curious to know why there is this smell of smoke
although there is no fire. A piece of an old kite

is hanging on the fence. A mist drifts through a mist.
I'm not there any longer, yet I'm all there: standing still.

Going and coming

Here is how we could sum it all up. A man is at home. His son is not here.
His daughter-in-law is staying with him for the time being. She
goes out. Comes back. She has someone in the meantime. He's doing well,
sleeps with her when he's free, a smart lad, who comes and goes.

A man is sitting at his desk. It is night. All is quiet. His son
is not here. On the sideboard place mats, lace doilies, and two
photographs. Sea at the window. Brown furniture. Tonight
he has to check some accounts. What balances. What doesn't.

A widow with bobbed hair was here earlier this evening,
almost by chance, she drops in now and then for a glass
of tea. The winter is passing. The sea remains. As for the light,
it goes and it comes. Now like this and now like that.

Tonight he needs to work out his profits and losses, what
does it profit a man. Rows of columns. Sorrow is not
like this: it has no measure. The carpenter is dead. The desk
is still here. The Narrator is running his fingers over it.

He's told the story of himself, and of his mother, he's tried to avoid
the word "like." He's told the tale of a wandering Russian merchant
who did not reach China and would never see his home again.
The tale of a snowman that roams alone among the rugged

mountains; he's told of the sea and of Chandartal. It revolves,
the whole business, it comes and it goes. The moon tonight
is pale and sharp, frightening the garden, twisting the fence,
tapping lightly on your window: now please begin all over again.

Silence

Even you. Everyone. All Bat Yam will be full of new people and they
in their turn, all alone in the night, will wonder at times with surprise what
the moon is doing to the sea and what is the purpose of silence. And they too
will have no reply. All of this hangs more or less on a thread. The purpose
of silence is silence.

Draws in, fills, heaves

And now it's as clear as can be. The moon is bending low over the dark of the sea, drawing up toward itself expanses of many waters and the mighty waves of the deep, covering them as if with lead. All over the sea the moon spreads a quicksilver web which it draws in and heaves up to itself. That is what I am talking about.

At journey's end

Now he is resting up in a cheap inn in a small town in the south
of Sri Lanka. Through the crisscrossed bars three huts, a slope,
little sailing boats, the Indian Ocean, warm, its waves are sharp
slivers of green bottleglass in the harsh sun. Maria is not here. She
has gone to Goa, from where she may return to Portugal. Or
she may not. It's hard for her. In the tiny cell is a stool, a rusty nail,
a hanger, a yellow rush mat, and in the corner a mattress.
There is a cracked washbasin whose enamel surface is scarred by black
patches. A nibbled electric wire curls slackly along the walls, draped
in cobwebs. A hotplate stained brown by milk that has boiled over
and not been cleaned for years. And there is a picture cut out of a
magazine, showing the Queen of England, with an air of faint distaste,
bending and patting the head of an almost crying local child, his shabby
trousers drooping, his limbs gaunt, a starving alley-cat.
The picture is dotted with fly droppings. And there is a cracked sink,
and a tap leaking rusty water drop by drop. Lie down now on
the mattress and listen. You've been here and there, you've sought
and you've found, this is the place. And when the daylight fades,
when the damp tropical evening smothers this glassy light, you
will still lie on this mattress, sweating and listening, not
missing a drop. And in the night too, and tomorrow: drop drop
drop and this is Xanadu. You've arrived. Here you are.

Here

Moon in the morning moon in the evening wreaking light in the night
skeletal all the day hurting every part O my child Absalom my son
my son Absalom, the desk is here the bed is here the guitar is here but
you are a dream moon in the night moon in the day glowing on the sea
pale in the window, preying on every living part my son my son.

What you have lost

Giggy Ben-Gal who had arrived back only the previous day from Brussels
drove in his new BMW to look at an old orange grove near Binyamina
that was about to be dug up. He had had a reliable tip that in a couple of years
this whole area would be released for housing. It would pay to snap up today
at the price of farmland what tomorrow would be prime building lots in a
sought-after district. He sat till evening in a fairly run-down village house,
was offered thick coffee and home made carob jam, and had a jocular
conversation with the heirs of the deceased farmer. The younger son was
on the ball, he'd served in a crack regiment; the older son seemed rather
tricky, saying hardly a word, with one eye closed and the other only half
open, too mean to waste more than a quarter of a look on you.
Every time the conversation inched in the direction of a deal, he would throw
in a sour half-sentence. Forget it, mate. We weren't born yesterday either.
At last, as it was getting dark, Giggy stood up and said, Right, OK, let's
put it on hold, first the two of you try to sort out what game you're in, then
give me a call and we'll talk, here's my card. Instead of driving straight back
into town he decided to take another look at the orange grove that was dying
because it didn't pay to irrigate it. There was a giant ficus tree nearby,
bowed with age, and beneath it Giggy parked and walked down the rows
of orange trees, treading on thistles and whistling. Birds whose names he
didn't know replied from the branches, chattering, pleading, as though
they too were trying to sell him some marvelous piece of property
that they had no real idea of the value of, nor of its potential. For a quarter
of an hour he wandered, forcing his way through ferns and brambles until thick
darkness settled over the neglected grove and it was only with difficulty,
after getting lost, that he managed to locate his ficus tree, but his new BMW
had vanished with his cell phone inside it and all the birds fell silent all at once,

as though their singing had been no more than a cunning trick to lure
and distract him, so as to help the thief. Giggy was left all alone
in this out-of-the-way place where it was definitely not healthy to be alone
after dark, especially unarmed. He started to grope his way through the
undergrowth toward the village but the long low building he was heading for
turned out to be no more than an abandoned packing shed, and suddenly
a jackal or fox broke into a howl. Rather close. And in the distance dogs
barked and the darkness filled with stealthy movements. Giggy sat down
on the ground and leaned back against the wall of the dilapidated shed,
sensing the stab of cold stars among the branches of the grove and the glow
of his watch and patches of shadow among the trees. For a few moments
he cursed, then he stopped. He felt calm. A cold, mute beauty, a deep wide
night was opening up before his eyes. Here and there large shadows looked
at him and a feminine breeze from the sea inserted its fine fingers between his
shirt and his skin and for a moment he felt that all this, breeze, branches,
stars, even the darkness itself, was staring at him as though patiently waiting
for some delayed coin to drop. The dead farmer's house where he had spent
most of the day, with its two palm trees in front, suddenly
struck him as perfect for *Nirit's Love*: the cypresses all round the yard,
the tumbledown henhouses, the stacks of utility furniture,
the flower-patterned plaster all stained, the plywood and formica surfaces
blistered and peeling at the edges, this was the perfect location.
And now he opened himself up to hear the prickly carpet of crickets
and a cow lowing in the dark as though it was his own soul keening and
village women in the distance answered with a heart-rending Russian tune
the like of which you would never hear again in Tel Aviv. Arise now and
go, light and calm get up and go in search of what you have lost.

Translator's Note

The Same Sea is replete with allusions to the Bible, the rabbinic writings and modern Hebrew literature. It is not essential to its reading to be able to identify and locate all these allusions, and I felt that to indicate them all by means of footnotes would interfere with the reader's enjoyment, but I offer here the references of some of the recurrent biblical allusions, particularly those which might otherwise seem puzzling. The commonest allusions, too frequent and generally familiar to be given here, are to the story of David, told in 1 and 2 Samuel and the beginning of 1 Kings. The two short texts, the Song of Songs (or Song of Solomon) and Ecclesiastes, are also alluded to, as are the Psalms and the Book of Job, in particular the following verses (all quoted from the Authorized King James version):

Song of Songs

1:15   Behold, thou art fair, my love; behold thou art fair; thou hast doves' eyes.

2:7   ...by the roes, and by the hinds of the field, that ye stir not up, nor awake my love, till he please.

2:9   My beloved is like a roe or a young hart: behold, he standeth behind our wall, he looketh forth at the windows, shewing himself through the lattice.

2:16   My beloved is mine, and I am his: he feedeth among the lilies.

5:1   I am come into my garden, my sister, my spouse: I have gathered my myrrh with my spice; I have eaten my honeycomb with my honey; I have drunk my wine with my milk...

5:2   I sleep, but my heart waketh: it is the voice of my beloved that knocketh, saying, Open to me, my sister, my love, my dove, my undefiled: for my head is filled with dew, and my locks with the drops of the night.

5:4 My beloved put in his hand by the hole of the door, and my bowels were moved for him.

5:5 I rose up to open to my beloved; and my hands dropped with myrrh and my fingers with sweet smelling myrrh, upon the handles of the lock.

8:7 Many waters cannot quench love, neither can the floods drown it: if a man would give all the substance of his house for love, it would utterly be contemned.

Ecclesiastes

1:2 Vanity of vanities, saith the Preacher, vanity of vanities; all is vanity.

1:3 What profit hath a man of all his labour which he taketh under the sun?

1:4 One generation passeth away, and another generation cometh: but the earth abideth for ever.

1:5 The sun also riseth, and the sun goeth down, and hasteth to his place where he arose.

1:6 The wind goeth toward the south, and turneth about unto the north; it whirleth about continually, and the wind returneth again according to his circuits.

1:7 All the rivers run into the sea; yet the sea is not full; unto the place from whence the rivers come, thither they return again.

1:8 All things are full of labour; man cannot utter it: the eye is not satisfied with seeing, nor the ear filled with hearing.

1:9 The thing that hath been, it is that which shall be; and that which is done is that which shall be done: and there is no new thing under the sun.

11:7 Truly the light is sweet, and a pleasant thing it is for the eyes to behold the sun:

11:8 But if a man live many years, and rejoice in them all; yet let him remember the days of darkness; for they shall be many. All that cometh is vanity.

Psalms

42:1 As the hart panteth after the water brooks, so panteth my soul after thee, O God.

Job

1:21 Naked came I out of my mother's womb, and naked shall I return thither: the Lord gave, and the Lord hath taketh away; blessed be the name of the Lord.

The New Testament allusions are mainly to the Gospels. Of the many references to post-biblical Hebrew literature I shall single out one which seems particularly relevant. It is a poem by Rahel (1890–1931):

Only of myself I know how to tell,
my world is as narrow as an ant's,
like an ant too my burden I carry,
too great and heavy for my frail shoulder.

My way too—like the ant's to the treetop—
is a way of pain and toil;
a gigantic hand, assured and malicious,
a mocking hand lies over all.

All my paths are made bleak and tearful
by the constant dread of this giant hand.
Why do you call to me, wondrous shores?
Why do you lie to me, distant lights?

Nicholas de Lange
Cambridge, May 2000

If you enjoyed reading *The Same Sea,*
look for these other titles by Amos Oz

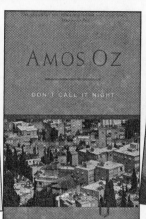

Panther in the Basement
0-15-600630-8
$11.00 (PB)

Don't Call It Night
0-15-600557-3
$11.00 (PB)

The Story Begins
0-15-100297-5
$20.00 (HC)

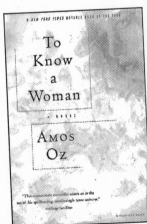

To Know a Woman
0-15-690680-5
$10.00 (PB)

Fima
0-15-600143-8
$13.00 (PB)

In the Land of Israel
0-15-648114-6
$13.00 (PB)